For Dr. Sam McKenna,

whose mission of healing

has touched my life

FOCUS ON THE FAMILY®

Christian Heritage Series

THE SANTA FE YEARS

The Mission

Nancy Rue

BETHANY HOUSE PUBLISHERS
MINNEAPOLIS, MINNESOTA 55438

A Focus on the Family book
Published by Bethany House Publishers
A Ministry of Bethany Fellowship International
11400 Hampshire Avenue South
Bloomington, Minnesota 55438
www.bethanyhouse.com

Printed in the United States of America by
Bethany Press International, Bloomington, Minnesota 55438

Library of Congress Cataloging-in-Publication Data

Rue, Nancy N.
   The mission / Nancy Rue.
     p.   cm. — (Christian heritage series, the Santa Fe years; bk. 4)
Summary: When Will's prayers for his father's return from the war are not
answered in the way he had hoped, he turns away from God and finds his
troubles only get worse.
   ISBN 1-56179-894-0
   1. World War, 1939–1945—United States—Juvenile fiction. [1. World
War, 1939–1945—United States—Fiction. 2. Prayer—Fiction. 3. Santa Fe
(N.M.)—Fiction. 4. Christian life—Fiction.] I. Title.
   PZ7.R88515 Mk   2001
   [Fic]—dc21   2001001919

1 2 3 4 5 6 7 8 9 10 11 12 13 14 15 / 08 07 06 05 04 03 02 01

*T*hat was the funniest movie I ever saw in my life," Fawn said. "I never laughed so hard."

Will Hutchinson, her foster brother, rolled his eyes at his friend Kenichi. "You said the same thing last Saturday, Fawn—*and* the Saturday before that, *and*—"

"They just keep getting funnier," Fawn said. "I saw you splitting your sides too. You laughed so hard, you spit in your peanuts."

"Did not!" Will said.

Fawn didn't hurl back a "did, too," but instead gave him a poke in the side and took off running down the carpeted stairs of the Lensic Theatre, dragging Kenichi's sister Emiko behind her. Emiko gave a crinkly-eyed grin over her shoulder.

"Hey!" Will said.

He started off after them, but Kenichi put his arm out. "Let 'em go," he said. "I've had enough of sisters today. They giggled all the way through the newsreel *and* the cartoon *and* the episode from the Captain America serial. They were in stitches before the movie even started. Why do they laugh at things that aren't even funny?"

"They're 10," Will said. "And they're girls. We're 12, and we're boys. There's your answer. Come on, we better get down there before they tear the lobby apart."

"Wait a minute," Kenichi said. "Where's Abe?"

Will looked back at the row of plush red seats they'd just vacated. Abe *hadn't* vacated his seat. The oversized 15-year-old was still sitting there, staring at the velvet curtains that had been drawn across the screen. Will grinned at Kenichi.

"Poor guy—we forgot to tell him it was time to go. He still hasn't seen that many movies—he doesn't exactly get it yet."

Will wiped the grin off as he hurried over to Abe. His friend was good-natured, but he got his feelings hurt if he thought people were laughing at him. Unfortunately, a lot of people did, which always got Will's hackles up and was enough to provoke Fawn into an all-out attack. As their mom always told them, Abe wasn't smart in the same way that other kids were smart, and he needed their protection from people who didn't understand that.

"Hey, pal," Will said to him. "The movie's over. We gotta go home."

Abe didn't take his eyes off the curtain. "Abey like talking camels."

"Yeah, they were pretty hilarious. Come on—"

"Bob Hope."

"Yep, Bob Hope, and Bing Crosby, and Dorothy Lamour." Will tousled Abe's butter-colored hair. "They say she's a luscious dish, that Dorothy Lamour."

Abe shook his head solemnly. "She princess."

"She was a princess in the movie—in *Road to Morocco*—but she's not really. She's just an actress. I'll explain it all to you on the way home."

"Abey wait for camels." Abe pointed to the curtain.

"They're not back there," Will said patiently. "They were just on the movie, and the movie's gone, see?" He didn't dare try to explain that those camels weren't really talking. They'd be there all night. As it was, the usher was going to come in any minute and boot them out of there.

"Where camels go?" Abe said.

Will groaned inside. *It's hard enough to figure out what he's talking about when he speaks English. If he starts in on German, forget it!*

"Hey," Will said, "I think we can get some more free peanuts if we hurry."

Abe gave his big, sloppy grin. "Abey like peanuts."

"I know you do, pal. It's food."

But even the lure of more snacks wasn't enough to keep Abe from looking back longingly at the closed curtains as Will tugged him gently toward the steps where Kenichi was waiting.

"So, Abe," Will said as he continued to push him ahead. "What was your favorite part?"

Abe puckered up his lips, then grinned down at his shoes.

"I get it," Kenichi said. "He liked it when Bob Hope kissed the girl and the toes of his shoes curled."

"Oh," Will said. "I wasn't too crazy about the kissing parts—or when Bing Crosby sang under her window."

"Yeah," Kenichi said, nodding toward the velveteen loveseat on the landing where Emi and Fawn were sitting, swinging their legs. "We got too many girls already."

"What I wouldn't give right now for one of those trick cigarettes they had—"

"Oh, yeah, or a whoopee cushion," Kenichi said. "We could get those girls good, couldn't we?"

Will grinned. "If the war was really like that, it wouldn't be so bad to be over there!"

"Dream on, kid."

Will looked up at a white-whiskered usher who was heading up the steps with his whisk broom and dustpan. He stopped just a few steps above Emiko and Fawn and glared up at the boys.

"You don't really think the war's a bunch of slapstick and playin' around in tents like you just seen in that movie, do ya?" the old usher said.

" 'Course not!" Will said. But he could feel himself sagging inside. For just a few minutes it had been kind of fun to imagine that the men overseas were having some laughs. *Who asked you to horn in on this conversation anyway?* Will wanted to say. But he ran his hand up and down the polished banister and hoped the old guy would head on up the stairs.

No such luck. Usher Man leaned against the brocade-covered wall and comfortably crossed the whisk broom and dustpan in front of him as if he intended to stay awhile. Will could see Fawn inching toward the edge of her seat for takeoff.

"Did you kids get in free?" Usher Man said.

"Yeah," Will said. "Both our moms bought war bonds."

"Yours, too?" he said to Fawn.

"Me and her have the same mom, sort of—" Will started to say.

"Did you know your people have purchased over $50 million in war bonds so far?" Usher Man said to Fawn.

"What do you mean, my people?" Fawn said. Will groaned inwardly again. He could see the storm gathering in her eyes.

"The Indians. I know you people like to be recognized by tribe and all that, but this report I heard just said all the Indians. Now, that's somethin' to be proud of."

Will knew Fawn wasn't. Although she was part Navajo and part Tanoan, what she really wanted to be was an Anglo, like him.

"Anyways," the old man went on before Fawn even had a chance to get riled, "I commend your parents for buyin' bonds.

Now, do you know *why* they bought them?"

Will's mom was buying them so Dad could start his own art studio and gallery when he came home from the war, but Will didn't feel like telling this busybody that. The man was beginning to get on his nerves.

I wish I could just make like Bob and Bing and hightail it out of here, he thought. It was about the hundredth time in the last few weeks that he'd felt the urge to get away from people lecturing him, telling him what to do. *Yeah, I wish I was "on the road"—to anywhere!*

"They're buyin' them," Usher Man was droning on, "to help with the war effort. Now, what does that mean, exactly?"

Fawn was by this time in a crouched position, and Emiko was doing the same. Will had to get this conversation over with.

"It means so the government can buy food and supplies and ammunition and build more ships and planes," Will said. "We really gotta go—"

"Right, sonny. Not for whoopee cushions and harem pants and trick cigarettes. They're not playin' a game over there—"

"I *know*," Will said, hackles starting to rise. "My dad is a prisoner of war in the Philippines. Her dad is in the signal corps, right in the middle of Germany. Their dad—" he pointed to Kenichi and Emiko, "is in China translating Japanese documents for the army. And his dad—" he jerked his head toward a now very pale Abe, "might not even be alive because he's in one of Hitler's concentrations camps. We *know* it isn't a game!"

Usher Man blinked. "Well! There's no need to get sassy about it."

Will thought there was *every* need, but he buttoned his lip. Fawn, however, was past buttoning hers. While Emiko and Kenichi politely looked at the floor, and Abe stuck his fist in his mouth and whimpered under his breath, she stood up, hands on hips, and tossed her black pigtails over her shoulders.

"We listen to the radio, too, Mister," she said. "And we heard that the war's gonna be over by Christmas, and that's only 10 days away—so there!"

Will exchanged a look with Kenichi which clearly said, "Sisters!" Any minute, he thought, the usher was going to ask them to leave, voice cold, whiskers going wild.

But Usher Man just stroked his grizzly beard, and then he laughed.

"You're naïve, Missy," he said, "and the rest of you, too, if you believe that."

"What's naïve mean?" Will said.

"It means you're so innocent and young, you'll believe anything you hear as long as it's what you *want* to hear. We're not going to declare victory until the Axis powers—Japan, Germany, and Italy—surrender unconditionally, and how's that going to happen in less than two weeks?" The laugh, rough as sandpaper, erupted again. "Don't expect anybody home for at least another year."

"You're a liar!" Fawn cried.

Her black eyes were snapping, and Will knew what that meant. But before he could think his next thought, she had already sprung from the bench and hurled herself on Usher Man's back.

"Hey—what in blazes!" the man said. He bent almost double and turned himself around, first one way, then the other, trying to shake her off. But Fawn had a firm hold on him with both knees and one hand while she pounded on him with the other.

Emiko scrambled off the seat and hid behind Abe, who was by now trying to stuff both fists into his mouth. Will jerked his head at Kenichi, and the two of them grabbed Fawn by the shoulders and peeled her away from Usher Man's back. She set up a howl and clawed the air, but Kenichi got both of his arms around her and pinned her against him. Will clapped a hand over her mouth.

"What's going on here?" said yet another voice, this time from the lobby below. It had to be the theater manager, Will thought. He was wearing a suit and carrying a pot of poinsettias, which he set on the carpet before he hurried up the stairs.

"This girl jumped me!" the old man said, voice cracking.

The manager cocked an eyebrow at the fuming Fawn. "This little thing?" he said.

"She may be little, but she packs a powerful wallop. I think she broke my back!"

"He started it, though," Will said. "He was sayin' stuff about the war draggin' on, and she's got a dad over there. We all do."

"I was just speakin' the truth," Usher Man said. He put his hand on the small of his back and slowly straightened up. "Kids these days are—"

"Kids these days are as on edge as everybody else," the manager said. "I've seen tempers flare over less than this." He turned to Will. "You and your friends go on home now. And have the little Indian princess here hit a punching bag or something. I don't have ushers to spare."

Will was more than happy to nod everybody down the steps and follow at a half-gallop himself.

"Fawn not princess," Abe whispered to him as they hurried across the lobby. "Dorothy lady—she princess."

"You got that right," Will muttered back. Fawn was definitely no princess.

When they stepped outside the Lensic, the sidewalks were jammed with Santa Fe Christmas shoppers, and Will kept a close eye on Fawn when Kenichi let her go. If she got loose in this crowd with that burr under her saddle, as Mom always called something that triggered Fawn's temper, there was no telling what she might do. Emiko was talking to her, though, and that always calmed Fawn down. Fawn had had no girlfriends at all, until she met Emiko. That was when the Hutchinsons had helped Abe's almost-adopted father get Kenichi and Emiko and their mother and brother out of the Japanese relocation camp just outside Santa Fe. As far as Will was concerned, Fawn was turning into a wild thing. Emiko, Mom said, was a good influence on her, even though she was pretty feisty herself. As for Kenichi, Will had never had a better friend.

The two of them and Abe trailed the girls into the Plaza, the four-sided park in the middle of the town. The Plaza was surrounded on three sides by stores and shops and restaurants, and on the Palace Avenue side by the long, low Governor's Palace. Even under its portico, as cold as it was, the Indian women who squatted there with their wares were surrounded by buyers dickering for pottery and jewelry and trinkets. There was a fog of breaths coming out of people's mouths.

It was late afternoon and the sky was watercolored with thin clouds—ready, Will knew, for a spectacular sunset. The crisp winter air was heavy with piñon smoke coming from wood stoves and kiva fireplaces. At the end of San Francisco Street, the bells of St. Francis Cathedral were chiming "God Rest Ye Merry, Gentlemen."

It feels like Christmas, he thought. *But then, it doesn't. Not without Dad here. Again. This is the fourth one.*

"That fella was wrong," he said out loud.

"Who, that usher person?" Fawn said. "Of course he was wrong. The war is going to be over by Christmas and all our dads are gonna be home and that's that."

"I don't know, Fawn," Kenichi said. "It's less than two weeks away, and they haven't even gotten all the way through Germany yet."

"Ugh. I wish we could go over there and hurry it up!" she said.

Emiko gave her soft bell of a laugh. "I bet you could, Fawn."

"If they saw you coming, they'd all run," Kenichi said.

Will could see Fawn's face clouding over. He quickly put himself in front of her and walked backwards as he talked.

"We can't give up hope, that's what Mom says. We just gotta keep prayin' and doin' what we're doin'."

"It's not helping," Fawn said, chin set.

The rest of them nodded in agreement, including Abe. It was a dismal sight.

"Hey, snap out of it, see?" Will said. "Why the long faces, see? We gotta liven this party up!"

"You sound just like Bob Hope, Will!" Emiko said. "Doesn't he? I think he does."

"Do some more, Willie," Kenichi said.

"All right—look around you, ya knuckleheads. You ever seen so many *farolitos* in your life?"

"What's a *farolito*?" Kenichi said.

Will pointed to the paper bags which lined the three flat roof levels of the LaFonda Hotel they were standing in front of. Each contained a bed of sand and a votive candle which would be lit at sundown. It was one of Will's favorite things about Christmas in New Mexico, the way they gave off a magical glow when they were all lit—to welcome the Christ Child, the natives said.

"Wait'll they're all lit, see?" Will said, talking out of the side of his mouth, Bob Hope style, as he continued to lead the way backwards. "It'll knock your socks off, I'll tell ya. So no more gloomy gusses, see? I wanna see smiles from now on."

Suddenly Kenichi's face startled out of its smile and he called out, "Willie, watch it!"

But it was too late. Will felt himself backing into something soft and sweet-smelling, and when he flailed to keep his balance, his hand slid off of silk like it was going down a slide at the park.

"Excuse me!" he said before he saw who he'd run into. But when he did, his mouth froze.

He was looking up into the "luscious" face of Dorothy Lamour.

✠ ⁃✠⁃ ✠

Chapter Two

*H*ey, handsome," said the deep, rich voice Will knew so well. "Been walking long?"

Several different answers flipped through Will's mind, but all he could do was stare into her wide-set eyes.

"Not talking yet, huh?" she said.

"Um—yeah—I mean—I'm sorry—"

"Don't worry, honey," she purred. "You'll catch on with a little practice."

By now, Will knew his face was red all the way to the roots of his almost-blond hair. He could feel the tips of his ears burning.

"Look at those blue eyes, honey," she said. "You are gonna be a looker when you get older. You just need to learn to face forward when you're walking if you're going to impress the girls; isn't that right, ladies?"

Fawn and Emiko nodded, Emiko gurgling like a boiling pot. Even Kenichi had a lopsided grin, and Abe's mouth was hanging so far open, Will could nearly see his tonsils. If there was ever a starstruck group, he thought, they were it.

Will cleared his throat. "Uh, I'm sorry I ran into you. I shoulda been lookin' where I was goin'.""

Miss Lamour tilted her head, and for the first time Will noticed that all of her hair was tucked away into a hair net. Just a half hour before, it had been tumbling down her back in curls on the big screen at the Lensic. Suddenly all he could think of was the cowlick that stuck out the top of his own head.

"Now that *is* true," she said. "You did nearly plow me down right here on the sidewalk. What are you going to do about it?"

"Uh—are you hurt or something? I could maybe call a doctor—"

Will stopped, because she put her hand on his sleeve. He could practically feel the cowlick growing to the size of a rooster tail, and his arms looking longer and lankier by the second, and his head looking too big for his skinny body—because beautiful Dorothy Lamour, the movie star, was leaning on his arm.

"I have the perfect solution, honey," she said.

"Yeah?" Will said.

"The only way you're going to make this up to me is to be my guest at the show tonight. You and your friends here."

"What show?" Fawn said.

For once, Will was glad she'd opened her mouth. His was frozen.

"You haven't heard of the Stars Over America Cavalcade?" Miss Lamour said. "Honey, we're traveling all over the country, visiting communities and selling war bonds." Her eyes twinkled. "You've heard of war bonds, now, haven't you?"

"Oh, yeah!" Fawn said. "Our moms buy 'em all the time."

"All time!" They all looked at Abe, who was clapping his big hands and bobbing his head. "You princess!" he said.

Will started to explain that they'd just seen *Road to Morocco*, but Miss Lamour gave his arm a little squeeze.

"I want you to promise you'll bring this big fella tonight, now, you hear?" she said.

Will was pretty sure a whole herd of talking camels couldn't have kept Abe away.

"Now, you'll have to ask your parents, of course," Miss Lamour said. "And I'll have tickets waiting for you at the box office. Just come to St. Michael's Gymnasium by seven o'clock. What's your name, handsome? I'll have them set aside for you."

Will blinked. She was talking to him. Emiko and Fawn went into a fit of giggles, and Ken put his hand over his mouth. Will was sure it was to cover the grin that was certain to get him pounded. Abe, of course, just bobbed gleefully and stared at his "princess."

"Your name?" Miss Lamour said. "Or should I just write 'Honey' on the envelope?"

"Do that!" Fawn said.

Will scowled at her. "It's Will," he said. "Will Hutchinson."

"Now there's a man's name," she said. "All right, Mr. Will Hutchinson, there will be tickets for all of you, and your parents." She gave his arm another squeeze before she let go. "I'm sure glad there are some of you who are still too young to be drafted."

They all stood there, still staring and giggling and bobbing, as she turned and hurried off down the sidewalk, right there on East San Francisco Street in Santa Fe. Fawn was the first to recover.

"Jeepers!" she said. "Wait'll Mama Hutchie hears about this!" And she took off toward St. Francis Cathedral at a dead run.

Will wasn't far behind her, though he did take time to call out over his shoulder, "See you at seven! Make sure Abe gets home!"

"All right, 'honey,'" Kenichi called back.

If he hadn't wanted to get home right behind Fawn so he

could at least tell Mom some of the details himself, Will would have stopped and wrestled Kenichi to the ground. But as it was, Fawn was already racing across the vacant lot on the corner of Cathedral Place and Castillo. By the time they crossed the bridge over the now-frozen ribbon of a river and headed up Canyon Road, Will was gasping for air. Fawn was still going strong.

Hey, wait a minute, he thought, as his side started to ache, *Mom's not even home yet. She said she was gonna be wrapping bandages for the Red Cross 'til six o'clock.*

With a smirk he slowed down and let Fawn plow through the slushy puddles ahead of him. But when their two-story territorial-style house came into view, there was a lamp on in the living room, and Mom's motorcycle was parked in the driveway. Will put on a burst of speed and careened into the kitchen only seconds after Fawn.

There were no smells of beans or tamales wafting from the stove, however. It was strangely quiet, and even Fawn was standing motionless in the doorway to the dining room.

"What are you doing?" Will said. "Where's Mom?"

Fawn pointed. Mom was in the living room, curled up in an overstuffed chair next to the fireplace, staring into it. There was no fire there.

Fear coursed through Will like he'd just opened a dam, and his eyes searched the room for a yellow piece of paper—a telegram. Only bad news could make Mom sit like that and do nothing. His mom never just did nothing.

"What's wrong with her?" Fawn whispered.

Will shook his head.

"Well, go find out!" she said.

She gave him a shove that pushed him out of the kitchen and out of the grip of panic. He went slowly toward Mom and scanned the room some more. No yellow paper.

"Mom?" he said.

She uncurled in the chair as if she'd been shot and put her hand to her chest.

"Good heavens, Will! You scared me half to death!" Her mouth twitched as she spotted Fawn. "Are you teaching him how to sneak up on me, Fawn?" she said. "Don't you think he's enough trouble as it is?"

Will felt himself sagging with relief. If Mom was almost smiling, that meant everything was okay. She wouldn't be doing that if she'd just gotten word that Dad was—well, it couldn't be bad.

"Come on, you two, sit down," Mom said. "I have news."

"What kinda news?" Fawn said. "I don't wanna hear it if it's bad."

She was already backing toward the dining room, but Mom shook her head. "No," she said, "for once it's good—or at least, it could be. Sit. Both of you."

Fawn plopped down on the floor, and Will went for the window seat.

"I was on my way out to the Red Cross," Mom said, "when your Uncle Al called."

Will went panicky again. Long distance? *Nobody calls long distance unless it's an emergency. We're supposed to keep the lines open for the military.* Three years of living with war had taught him that much.

"Now, don't bust a gasket," Mom said. "Uncle Al wanted to let me know about something that *might* have happened—a good thing."

"Like *what* good thing?" Fawn said.

It had to be about Dad. Uncle Al was in an intelligence unit. He knew things ordinary people didn't get to find out. He was the one who had told them Dad was in a Japanese prison camp for sure—

"I don't know if I wanna hear this, Mom," Will said.

"I think you do," she said. "Uncle Al says some American

prisoners have been rescued from a Japanese ship in the Philippines. Apparently they were being transported from a prison camp to Japan when a U.S. ship overtook their ship."

"Is one of them Will's dad?" Fawn said. "I bet it is, huh?"

"We don't know," Mom said. "Al is trying to get a list of the names of the rescued men, and he'll let us know as soon as he finds out. Will—Son, are you all right?"

Will didn't answer, because he didn't know *what* he was. After the long years of waiting, since he was nine years old, this was the first light-speck of real hope that his dad might be coming home, and he didn't know what to feel. He just shook his head.

"Fawn," he heard Mom say, "why don't you put some cookies on a plate and pour some milk? We'll be right in."

For once Fawn didn't argue. Mom came across the living room and sat next to Will on the window seat. She tapped his forehead.

"What's going on in there?" she said. "I can almost hear the wheels turning."

"Do you think he's one of 'em, Mom?" Will said. "I mean, really? Be honest."

"I don't know how to be anything else," she said. "But it's like there's a line drawn right down the middle of me. This half of me believes your father is on his way home to us right this very minute. This half is afraid to even think that—afraid we'll be disappointed."

"Yeah," Will said.

"But I've learned one thing from all this, and that's that you can't walk around split down the middle or you don't know if you're coming or going. Right?"

Will nodded.

"So we have to get pulled together, and I only know one way to do that."

"You're gonna say we should pray, huh?"

"My son is a genius, and he gets it all from his mother. I'm going to call Tina and Bud and the Lins to come over here and pray with us. Anybody else you want to invite?"

"Mr. T.," Will said.

Mom's mouth twitched. "Only in this bizarre lifetime would my kid volunteer to have his school principal come over."

She tousled his cowlick, and Will started to pull away like he usually did—when he remembered.

"Dorothy Lamour!" he said.

"All right," Mom said slowly. "We could invite her, only I don't think I have her number, Son." Her mouth twitched.

"No—I don't want to invite *her*—*she* invited *us*—"

"Dorothy Lamour invited you to pray?"

"No, she invited us to her show—tonight. That Star Cavalcade thing," Will said.

"Oh, the Stars Over America show at St. Michael's Gym. You're telling me she gave you a personal invitation? I think you've been seeing too many 'On the Road' movies."

"No, Mo-om! Listen!"

He managed then to get the story out while Mom's eyes got wider and wider. He was on the last part, where Dorothy Lamour walked away, when Fawn burst into the room.

"You told her the whole thing? Without me?" she said.

"Don't worry, Fawn," Mom said. "I'm sure he left out some important details. He's male, remember? They never think the little things are as vital as they really are."

Fawn's face grew sly. "Did he tell you that she kept calling him 'honey' and told him he was handsome?"

Mom broke into one of her rare smiles. "No," she said, raising both eyebrows at Will. "Well, a genius and handsome, too. There will be no living with you."

"Knock it off, Fawn!" Will said. He was sure even the roots of his hair were red this time. "Besides, we can't go to the show now anyway. We gotta stay here and wait for news about Dad."

The smile immediately disappeared from Mom's face, and she took him by both shoulders.

"Now listen to me, Will," she said. "I don't want you to give up every little piece of fun that comes your way because of this lousy war. It could be days, maybe even a week before Uncle Al knows anything for sure. Your father doesn't want you to miss wonderful things like this—I know he doesn't."

"It won't be any fun, though," Will said. "I'll be thinkin' about Dad the whole time—"

"No, you will not." Mom's face was more serious than Will had ever seen it. She looked right into his eyes, so hard he couldn't pull his away. "You have already sacrificed more than a kid your age should have to. Most of your childhood has been taken from you. I can't change that, but I can insist that you grab whatever parts of it you can and run with them."

"But, Mom—"

"Nope—end of discussion. I'm going to go make some phone calls. You two have some cookies. Fawn, what are you going to wear to the show?"

They faded off into the kitchen, talking about the wool jersey with white polka dots versus the brown wool with the woolen gaiters. Will sank onto the window seat.

If I'm supposed to be a kid grabbing fun, he thought, *how come I don't feel like one all of a sudden?*

All he *could* feel were his hackles going up. He had to watch out for Fawn and Abe all the time. He had to do his homework and not get in trouble so he wouldn't add to Mom's worries. He had to do a lot of stuff Dad would do if he were there—get firewood and carry out the trash. He was doing man things—and even Dorothy Lamour had practically come right out and said he was a man. But he was supposed to be a kid, too?

Going out on the road somewhere, anywhere, was sounding better by the minute.

Within half an hour, Pastor Bud and his wife, Tina, were there—with Abe, of course. Not long after that Emiko and Kenichi arrived with their big brother, Yoji, and their mother, Mrs. Lin. When Mr. T.—Mr. Tarantino, the principal of Will and Kenichi's junior high—arrived, the living room was so full, Emiko had to sit on Yoji's lap. Will told Fawn she'd better not even think about sitting on his. She told him she'd rather have chicken pox.

"I'm sure glad you called, Ingrid," Pastor Bud said to Mom. "I'd hate to see the Hutchinsons going through this thing alone." He put a pudgy hand on the back of Will's neck. "I know you have the man of your house here, but at times like this, even he needs some bolstering up."

Will tried not to stare. They were close friends, he and Bud; Bud was like a substitute father to him while his own was gone. But had they gotten so close Bud was reading his mind?

"Let's pray that the real man of the house is on that ship," Mom said, "so this one can be a kid like he's supposed to be."

Will's hackles started to come up, but Bud was grabbing his hand on one side and Mr. T. was doing the same on the other and everybody was bowing heads. He pushed the prickly feeling aside for the moment.

"Lord," Bud was saying, "during this war, one single ideal has moved our nation—the preservation of democracy, so that kids like Yoji and Kenichi and Emiko and Fawn and Will and Abe can grow up to be whatever You want them to be. We're asking to-night that part of that preservation will be the saving of men like Rudy Hutchinson and Choyo Lin and John McHorse—"

Fawn and Emiko, Will knew, would be squeezing each other's hands at the mention of Choyo Lin, Emiko's father, and John

McHorse, Fawn's. Will shut his eyes tighter and prayed hard for the name of Rudy Hutchinson.

Please bring him home, God. Please make him be one of the rescued men on that ship. Please make him be safe and get him back here—maybe even before Christmas if that's not too much to ask.

Bud's voice wove back into his thoughts, and Will listened. It was hard to believe he'd once thought Bud looked and sounded like Elmer Fudd. Right now he sounded as if God were right in front of him, hearing every word.

"Hear the prayers of Your people, our Father," Bud said, "and give us strength and patience to do Your will."

There was quiet for a few minutes, and then Mom put in a prayer, and then Tina. Pretty soon, everybody was asking God for a special piece of the puzzle that would bring the end of the war.

Mr. T. was last to pray. "Lord God," he said, "whatever the answers are to these prayers, help us to accept them with faith, knowing that You, and only You, are the author of peace."

Everybody murmured, "Amen," except Will.

What does he mean, "whatever the answers are"? he thought. *We've prayed hard here tonight. God's gonna give us what we need—He always does.*

He could feel it—in the thick, soft strength of Bud's hand. In the sinewy toughness of Mr. T.'s. In the grin Fawn sent him from across the circle. In the gurgle that came from Abe's throat.

God's here, he thought. *He'll give us what we asked for.*

"It's like a warm blanket, isn't it—praying like this?" Mom said.

"You feel better, Ingrid?" Tina said, as she fussed with Abe's hair.

"Much. I'm positive—and I'm peaceful."

"Does that mean you're going to go in the kitchen and rustle up some of your strudel?" Mr. T. said. His weather-hardened tan face crinkled into a grin. "I was afraid I was going to have to take everybody out to eat."

"Not the kids," Mom said. "They have a special invitation for the Stars Over America show."

"Dorothy Lamour invited us herself!" Fawn said, and then gave Will a triumphant look. She'd beaten him to it this time.

Mr. T. looked impressed. "Dorothy Lamour, huh? Who wangled that?"

Before Fawn could start going on about her calling him "handsome" and "honey," Will started for the coat closet and said, "We better get a move on or we'll be late."

Amid the shuffle that went on behind him, Mom managed to get to Will by the closet.

"Have the best time you can," she said. "Let me do the worrying about your dad."

"But there's no need to worry, Mom," Will said. "You were right about the praying. Dad's coming home—I know it."

She looked at him for a long minute, and then she smoothed down his cowlick. "I like your faith," she said. "I think I'll adopt you."

Her lips twitched and she stuck out her pinkie for him to link his to it—their substitute for a kiss. Then Will put on his coat and went off to see Dorothy Lamour, without a hackle in sight.

✛ ✛ ✛

Chapter Three

*T*he gym at St. Michael's High School was packed with Santa Feans when the kids arrived. There were old Spanish señoras in rusty-black rebozo scarves. Wealthy Anglo and Spanish townspeople wearing minks or puffing cigars. There were even several Pueblo women wrapped in bright red blankets, with cheeks nearly as rosy as their clothes from sitting in front of the Governor's Palace all day. One was clutching an envelope like Will's, so he knew she'd gotten free tickets, too.

The ones Will had, however, were for the front row of chairs, down on the floor, right in front of the portable stage, a fact that had Fawn and Emiko giggling before their seats even hit the chairs.

"You sit next to them, Abe," Ken said. "They're driving me batty."

"Not a very long drive, if you ask me," Fawn said, and then went off into gales of giggles with Emiko again.

Abe changed seats without a word, eyes cast down toward

the floor. The gurgling they'd heard from him all the way to St. Michael's was gone.

"What's wrong?" Will said to him. "Why the long face? I thought you were excited about seeing your 'princess'?"

He gave Abe a playful nudge, but Abe shook his head solemnly.

"Why not?" Will said.

"Bad boys," Abe muttered.

"What?"

"Bad boys here."

"What bad boys? They don't let bad boys come in here—"

But Will stopped. Abe was shaking his head hard, and there was a fear in his eyes Will hadn't seen since last summer, the last time they'd seen the Three Amigos: Luis and Pablo and Rafael.

"You don't mean Luis and those guys?" Will said.

Abe nodded and stuck his fist in his mouth.

"You didn't see them, Abe! They're in reform school!"

Abe took his hand out long enough to say, "They here," and then thrust it back in. Will twisted around in his seat and looked back over the sea of people in the direction Abe had pointed. He didn't see the three Mexican-American boys who had been a burr under Will's saddle from the time he'd started school in Santa Fe last spring until the judge had sent them off to be rehabilitated. They'd been worse than a burr for Abe.

He probably gets the heebie-jeebies every time he sees a Mexican kid, Will thought.

He reached up and patted Abe on the shoulder. "Get a load of these decorations, big fella."

They were definitely elaborate, and they turned out to be just the thing to get Abe's fist out of his mouth. Will found himself gaping right along with him.

The whole stage was festooned with red, white, and blue bunting, and there were lights flashing from every direction. STARS OVER AMERICA CAVALCADE was spelled out in silver letters that sparkled so brightly they hurt Will's eyes, yet he couldn't move them from the spectacle. You just didn't see things like this too often in New Mexico.

The band in the makeshift orchestra "pit" right in front of them suddenly struck up, and the gym was filled with trumpet and saxophone and trombone and clarinet sounds, all to the beat of a set of drums bigger than Will's whole bedroom. He could feel the music as much as hear it, and from the way Abe was keeping time with his head beside him, he was sure he was feeling it, too.

Then the footlights came up and the stage was alive with dancers in spangles, the colors flashing with every pass of the lights.

"Hey," Kenichi hissed in his ear, "that's Loretta Young."

"Nuh-uh," Will said. No sooner had the words crossed his lips than he caught sight of Rita Hayworth.

"Greer Garson!" Fawn said out loud.

The audience burst into applause, and Will had to concentrate to keep clapping. All he could do was stare, mouth open, letting drool escape from both corners. These were the stars he'd been watching in movies since he was old enough to sit up in a theater—and there they were, not 10 feet from him, smiling and singing and breathing the same air.

"I didn't know all *these* people were gonna be in it!" Kenichi whispered to him.

"Me neither!" Will said. "Look at Abe!"

Poor Abe looked overwhelmed. His mouth *was* hanging open, and the big cheeks were flushed with pure delight. And when Dorothy Lamour came to the microphone at the center of the stage, he nearly pitched forward out of his seat.

"Princess," he murmured.

Kenichi and Will grinned at each other.

"Welcome to the Stars Over America Cavalcade!" Miss Lamour

said. "Get ready for the show of a lifetime—*and* get ready to dig deep into those pockets and *buy bonds!*"

The whole troupe broke into "Take It Or Leave It," and from there it was an hour and a half of nonstop singing and dancing and joke-telling that kept Will leaned forward in his own seat. He had to remind himself to breathe.

Every few minutes there was a reminder to buy bonds. A man named Phil Baker, who was the emcee, came out each time and got the audience riled up.

"In Chicago, we raised $40,000," he told the audience. "Wanna know how we did it?"

"Yes!" cried the audience, as if they were one person.

"We auctioned off Betty Grable's nylon stockings!"

"Who's Betty Grable?" Kenichi whispered to Will.

"She's some lady with legs everybody goes nuts over," Will said.

"Yuck," Kenichi said.

Will agreed.

"But you don't need Betty's lingerie to raise money for bonds," Phil Baker went on. "In Peoria, a bunch of fellas went out on a raft and refused to come in until the community raised $5,000 to buy bonds!"

Once again the audience roared. Fawn leaned across Abe and said, "We could do that, Will!"

"Where are we gonna put a raft?" Will said. The Rio Grande was right now a ribbon of ice about a foot wide. He rolled his eyes at Kenichi.

"The list goes on," Phil Baker said. "And here to give you some more ideas is our own Dorothy Lamour!"

That brought Abe straight up out of his seat. He was on his feet, clapping madly as Miss Lamour sailed out onto the stage in a white gown that swirled around her like a hundred veils.

"She just had that one on in the movie today!" Fawn whispered.

Will wasn't as interested in the dress as he was in getting Abe to sit. People behind them were already hissing, "Down in front!"

He finally gave Abe's shirt a yank and got him heading backwards, but it was too late. Miss Lamour had already spotted him with her big, brown eyes, and to Will's horror, she was beckoning him with her finger.

"Come on up here, honey!" she said. "And bring all your friends."

Fawn and Emiko couldn't get to the stage fast enough, and Abe would have plowed straight through the orchestra if Will hadn't kept a firm grip on his shirttail, which was by now hanging out of his pants. Will looked at Kenichi. He was slumped down in his seat as far as he could go.

"No hiding, now," Miss Lamour said. "I want all of you up here—Will Hutchinson and all of his friends!"

The crowd was by now laughing and clapping and stomping its feet, and Will knew that to try to escape under the seat or up the aisle would have brought on a riot. But he wasn't going up there without support. He grabbed Kenichi's arm and dragged him with him, up to the stage.

"Here we are!" Miss Lamour said, stretching out her veil-clad arms to pull them all in close to her. The reflection from the jeweled bracelets on both arms nearly blinded Will. "These are some friends I met today, and I want to introduce them to you." She pointed to Fawn, who, amid a fit of giggles, said, "Fawn McHorse."

At the point of Miss Lamour's finger, they each said their names, even Abe, who gurgled out "Abey!" and almost brought down the house. When they'd all identified themselves except for Will, Miss Lamour put her hand on his arm and said, "Now I want you to meet a young man who knocked me off my feet this afternoon!"

The audience hooted and whistled, while Will felt his face going scarlet. Where was the nearest exit? Maybe he could tell her he had to go to the bathroom—no, that would make it worse.

"Mr. Will Hutchinson, ladies and gentlemen! Isn't he handsome?"

Okay, maybe the bathroom thing would *work after all*, Will thought, as the audience went wild and he looked for an exit. He caught a glimpse of Rita Hayworth's blonde head just offstage. There was no escape.

"I had to show off my friends," Miss Lamour was saying.

"Have them do a song with you!" somebody called out from backstage.

"A song? Would you like that, ladies and gentlemen?"

Evidently they did, because the biggest roar yet rose from the crowd. The band was already playing the introduction to "Over There."

"You know this one, don't you?" Miss Lamour said. "Everybody knows this one!"

Will *had* known it, until he'd found himself standing in front of several hundred people. Now he couldn't think of a single line.

"Over there!" Miss Lamour sang out. "Over there!"

To Will's amazement, Abe was warbling right along with her, every note and word right on. Fawn and Emiko could barely sing for giggling, and Kenichi was managing to croak out about every other word. He gave Will a poke in the ribs that helped him explode with—

"And it won't be over 'til it's over over there."

"That's right, ladies and gentlemen," Miss Lamour said, one arm slung around Abe's neck, the other around Will's. "We're close, but it ain't over yet. Our boys overseas still need our support, and the best way you can support them is to, let's hear it—"

She cupped her hand around her ear and the audience yelled, "BUY BONDS!"

Miss Lamour broke into a dance step then and nodded for the kids to join in. While Will was struggling to keep up, and hoping Abe wouldn't step on Miss Lamour's foot and cripple her for the rest of the crusade, a bright thought came into his head.

It's gonna be over soon—and my dad's gonna be home even sooner than that. *It* is *almost over for me.*

"Let's hear it for my friends up here!" Miss Lamour was shouting.

The audience went into another round of whistling and applauding, and Will started to make a beeline for his seat. But Miss Lamour caught him by the arm.

"One more thing," she said into his ear—which immediately went one shade of red darker.

"One more thing before I let them go!" she said to the audience. "We need to find out how much money *they* are going to raise for bonds. What's it gonna be, kids?"

She looked at Will, but before he could even calculate a figure, much less say it, Fawn jumped past Abe and Emiko and put her mouth right up to the microphone.

"We're gonna raise $500!" she said.

Are you nuts?! Will wanted to scream at her. He probably could have and never have been heard, the audience was going that wild.

"You heard it, folks!" Dorothy Lamour said. "And if these young people can pledge $500, I think you can come up with at least that much, don't you think? Come on—it's for our boys who are *where?*"

"Over there!" the crowd shouted.

The band struck up another chorus, and this time Miss

Lamour gave each one of the kids a kiss on the forehead and sent them back to their seats. Will thought he was going to have to carry Abe down. He was practically swooning.

"Aren't they cute, folks?" Miss Lamour said when they'd gotten back to the front row.

"Oh, yeah, Fawn," Will whispered. "You're *real* cute."

The show ended not long after that, with all the stars on stage calling out, "Bye-bye! BUY BONDS!"

The audience was busy shouting it back when Will grabbed Abe and said, "Come on—let's get outa here."

"Don't you think she'll let us visit her in her dressing room?" Fawn said.

"No—and I don't *want* to visit her in her dressing room!"

"Why?"

"Because I wanna get outa here before people start asking me how I'm gonna raise $500, that's why!"

Fawn sniffed and gave the stage one last longing look before she and Emiko and Abe followed Will and Kenichi out of the gym and out onto College Street.

Although the air was thick with piñon pine smoke, it was also nose-burning cold, and Will and Fawn didn't take long to say good-bye to Emiko and Kenichi, who promised to see Abe safely home.

"See ya tomorrow in church," Kenichi said. "Are you gonna bring the $500 with you then?"

Will punched him in the shoulder, but he glared at Fawn. "I'm gonna sock *you* one of these days, too."

"You will not," she said as she and Will headed off through the Barrio, a small district of Santa Fe where some of the, as Mom always put it, less fortunate people lived. "Mama Hutchie would never let you hit a girl."

"What else am I supposed to do when you make me look like a moron in front of half the town?"

"How did I make you look like a moron?" Fawn said. "We could raise $500 so easy."

"You gonna tell me how? We don't have anybody's nylons to auction off."

"Shh!"

"Whatta ya mean, 'shh'? You got us into this—"

"No—shhhhh!"

Fawn reached up and put her hand over Will's mouth. He tried to pry it off, though it was pointless. She was little, but she was stronger than most *boys* he knew.

"I think somebody's following us!" she whispered.

He shook his head, and she took her hand away.

"Is this another one of your spy sightings?" Will said. "Just because we're not in the ritziest neighborhood—"

"Shhh—no—I mean it!"

She grabbed him by the wrist and pulled him around the corner from DeVargas Street to Old Santa Fe Trail and into the shadow of a cottonwood.

"Somebody's back there," she whispered. "I could hear 'em."

Will looked around at the adobe houses that stood in the darkness like hulking mounds of clay. They did look a little spooky in the dark, especially the ones with falling-down coyote fences made out of splintery old wood. It was enough to get any-body's imagination going.

"Come on," he said to her. "Nobody's back there. Besides, who would want to get us? We sure don't have any money."

Fawn wasn't convinced, he could tell. She kept looking back over her shoulder as they crossed to the other side of Santa Fe Trail and started past the San Miguel Mission.

"Cut it out," Will said. "You're gonna get *me* spooked in a minute. It was nothin'."

"Then what *did* I hear?"

"The wind."

"The wind. Do you hear any wind, Will? It dies down at night—there's not a breath stirring—ahhh!"

She let out a shriek that was equaled only by Will's, for suddenly they were face-to-face with two figures who had emerged as if from thin air.

Actually, they had come over the low stone wall that surrounded San Miguel Mission. Even in the long, dark shadow that was cast by the chapel's bell tower, Will could see who it was. Rafael and Pablo were within inches, their eyes glittering in the night.

It didn't take Will more than a second to register that Abe had been right and that if Rafael and Pablo were there, the third Amigo couldn't be far away. He whirled around, just in time to see Luis step across the street, arms folded. His walk was swaggery, and Will saw that he'd grown several inches while he was in reform school. But other than that, he didn't seem to have changed a bit. He definitely didn't look "reformed."

"Hey, An-glow," Luis said as he joined his two pals and stepped in front of them so that his nose was only an inch from Will's. He was so close, Will could see the cracks in his mean-sneering lips.

"Hey, Luis," Will said. His heart was pounding, but to his relief, his voice didn't show it. "I see you're back."

"Oh, I am back, An-glow, and you gonna be seein' a lot of me."

"Nah, I don't think so," Will said. "I got other friends now—"

"I weren't never your friend, An-glow."

"Yeah, I know. I was being sarcastic."

In the puzzled pause that followed, Fawn whispered, "Do you want me to jump one of 'em?"

Will shook his head. He'd seen Luis when he was ready for a fight, and he wasn't now. He was just talking big. *That* Will had learned how to handle.

"You still owe me, An-glow," Luis said. "For makin' a fool outa me in the stamp contest last spring—and for gettin' us thrown in jail last summer."

"You did that to yourselves," Will said. "I didn't make you steal—"

"Shut-up, An-glow! I don't wanna talk about that."

"You brought it up."

"Now I'm gonna bring somethin' else up. I'm gonna get back at you—and you set yourself up for it real good tonight."

"How?" Will said.

Luis took a step forward. Will would have been willing to bet before that he couldn't have gotten any closer, but now he was nearly eyebrow to eyebrow with Will. He was sure his eyes were going to cross.

"You told everybody you gonna raise a lotta money for bonds. But you can't. I already know you can't. And I'm gonna make sure everybody knows it."

Will tried not to look too relieved. *The war's gonna be over and nobody's gonna care,* he thought. *And besides, my dad's gonna be home soon, and then you're gonna be sorry you ever threatened me.*

By now, Will had to bite his lip to keep from smiling. A whole lot of things were changing with Dad coming home, and all of them were good.

"I'm gonna make a fool outa you, An-glow," Luis said, finally stepping back so Will could breathe without smelling hot chilies. "Just like you did to me."

"Good luck," Will said. He even stuck out his hand for Luis to shake it. He didn't, but he did look stunned. He stood there staring long enough for Will to nod to Fawn to follow him toward Canyon Road.

"You looked pretty brave, Will," Fawn said when they were out of earshot. "Maybe you're gettin' tough after all."

"Nah," Will said. He didn't add that you didn't have to be tough when you prayed and knew God was taking care of things. He just stuck his hands in his pockets and whistled the rest of the way home.

✝ ✝ ✝

Chapter Four

*T*he next morning, Will woke up to the phone ringing, and he was out of bed and downstairs before his eyes were all the way open. It could, after all, be Uncle Al.

But in the kitchen, Mom was saying, "Thanks, Bud. We'll be ready."

"Ready for what?" Will said hopefully.

"For him to pick us up for church. He says it's too cold for us to go on the motorcycle." Her mouth twitched. "Fawn would be warm in the sidecar, but you and I would freeze our behinds off."

Will sagged a little as he looked out the window in the kitchen door. There wasn't a cloud anywhere, and the sky was already a brilliant blue. It was so clear, he could see the Jemez Mountains in the distance, shimmering in ice and misty snow.

Dad'll be home soon to paint this, he reassured himself. *We just gotta keep praying.*

He did that in church that morning, when he normally would have been staring out the window. When the service was over, he had a strong feeling inside, as if he'd somehow grown taller in the last hour. It was the feeling of being sure.

That whole afternoon, he barely let the smile off his face. Even when he and Mom and Fawn had to trek across ground frozen hard as iron to get to Rios's Woodyard for firewood, crackling the brittle ice underfoot with the wheelbarrow, he was singing made-up verses of "Over There."

"You didn't sing that loud last night when we were on the stage," Fawn said.

"I didn't know then what I know now—not really," Will said.

Mom's lips twitched. "And what, pray tell, is that?"

"That Dad really has been rescued and he's coming home."

"Well, we certainly like to think—"

"No, Mom, I *know*. You're the one who's always telling me, you pray for the things you want and if you have enough faith, they'll come true."

"Oh," Fawn said, "you mean, like wishes?"

"No," Mom said. "Not like wishes." Her mouth had stopped twitching. "God isn't the fairy godmother, Will."

"Nope," Will said. "He's better. Hey, old Señor Rios raised his prices!"

It took a few seconds for Mom's eyes to pull away from Will's face to the sign which now read "Fill Up With Firewood—35 Cents."

"Didn't it used to be 25?" Will said.

"Yeah," Mom said. Her voice sounded vague for a moment before she looked back at Will and said, "We'll talk about this prayer thing later, all right?"

Will shrugged happily. Sure. He'd be glad to tell Mom anything she wanted to know about praying and faith.

They loaded up the wheelbarrow and picked a Christmas tree from the selection Jesus Rios had leaning against his shed.

"I know what let's do," Mom said. "Let's decorate it this week sometime and leave it up until Dad comes home—no matter how long it takes."

"Sure," Will said. "But it isn't gonna take that long."

Mom didn't answer.

Later that evening, after Will brought in a leather sling full of firewood from the pile they'd made outside and Fawn gathered up a black bucketful of kindling, Mom made a blazing fire in the kiva-style fireplace. It was a little painful for Will to look at it at first because of the memories. It was called a kiva because it was rounded like the sacred kivas found on the Indian pueblos. Will wasn't allowed to go to Fawn's family's pueblo, San Ildefonso, anymore because of an incident with their kiva. Although Fawn claimed it didn't bother *her* not to go there—because she wanted nothing more than to be considered an Anglo—it bothered Will. He really liked Fawn's grandfather, Quebi, and he missed talking to him.

But he shrugged right now as he watched the flames dance inside the kiva. *Pretty soon, Dad'll be home, and I can talk to him anytime I want to.* And there definitely was nobody better than his dad for that—not even Bud or Mr. T. Not even Quebi.

Mom cooked pinto bean soup in her bean pot right in the kiva and let them eat supper in the living room because nobody wanted to be far from the fire. She made cocoa afterwards and told them they could do their homework in front of the fireplace, just this once.

Fawn and Will sprawled out on their stomachs with their books on the big Navajo rug, and Mom took a chair right next to the kiva with *Time of Harvest*, which Will knew was set in New Mexico. For a Midwesterner, she was getting pretty attached to the Southwest. Will wondered if Dad would want to stay here when he came back.

"There is something wonderful about curling up in a chair by the fireplace with a cup of hot chocolate and a good book,"

Mom said. "You realize, of course, that I just used up the next month's supply of chocolate for this."

"We're not gonna have to ration much longer," Will said.

"Oh?" Mom said. "More inside information?"

"No, everybody knows the war's just about over."

"I don't know about that," Mom said, "but I sure could use some news."

"I'll turn on the radio," Fawn said.

Mom gave her almost-smile as Fawn scrambled up.

Not that kinda news, Fawn, Will thought. *News about Dad.*

He noticed that Mom hadn't turned a page in a while. She was nervous.

She's gotta pray more, he thought.

They were quiet for a while, listening to Edward R. Murrow report that the Soviets were pushing the Germans back on the eastern front—that the Allies in the Pacific were mobilizing to take Iwo Jima from Japan—that the Allies in the European Theatre were beginning what they were calling the Battle of the Bulge.

"They sure have weird names for stuff," Fawn said.

"That's probably where your dad is, Fawn," Mom said.

Fawn tilted her head over her geography book and fiddled with the end of one of her black pigtails. "You think my dad's gonna be home soon, too?"

"As soon as the war ends, yes," Mom said.

"And that's gonna be soon," Fawn said. She was looking at Will now. He didn't even hesitate.

"You heard what he just said on the radio: We're kicking the Germans' and the Japanese's tails all over the world now. Besides—weren't you payin' attention when we all prayed in here last night?"

"Kind of," Fawn said. "Only, I had to hold Abe's hand and it was sweaty and that was all I could think about."

Mom chuckled, but Will shook his head.

"You gotta get serious about it, Fawn. If you really want your dad to come home, you gotta pray really hard—and you gotta believe it's gonna happen."

"How do you know?" Fawn said, eyes narrowing suspiciously.

"I've seen it happen. You got to come live here. Tina and Bud get to adopt Abe. We got the Lins out of the relocation camp."

"Jeepers," Fawn said. "That was all because we prayed?"

"Let me just inject something here," Mom said. She closed the book and set it aside. "I'm glad that you're seeing all the good things that have happened to us in the last several months, and I'm glad you're giving God the credit. But—"

She didn't finish the sentence. The telephone jangled in the kitchen, and all three of them jerked their heads and then froze.

No "buts" about it, Will thought. *That's gotta be Uncle Al.*

But it was Margretta Dietrich. She was the lady who had helped Fawn and her mother, Frog Woman, when Fawn's father had gone off to the war. Frog Woman couldn't live *on* the pueblo because she had married outside her tribe, and it had become impossible for her to live *off* of it because she'd come down with a serious eye disease. Margretta had taken her to Arizona to be treated; they'd been there for six months.

Will tried not to show his disappointment that it wasn't news about Dad, especially when Mom covered the mouthpiece with her hand and said to Fawn, "Your mother's doing well! She's almost finished with her treatments." It was, after all, one thing they'd prayed for.

"See what happens when you really pray?" Will said.

Fawn scowled. "Yeah? And what's gonna happen now? When she comes back, am I gonna have to leave here? I didn't pray for that!"

"Would you two hush?" Mom hissed. "I'm on the phone here."

Fawn stomped off to the living room. *Poor kid*, Will thought. *There's sure a lot of stuff I gotta pray about.*

And the next day at school, it turned out there was more.

It was the period right after lunch, Mrs. Rodriguez's social studies class. Will, Kenichi, and their friend Neddie were passing out a new set of books for her while she took the roll. Neddie wore glasses and had a head that Will thought was about two sizes too big for his toothpicky body, but he had more imagination than any other three kids put together. He was pretending his stack of books was the Leaning Tower of Pisa, with Will and Kenichi looking on, when the classroom door opened. Everybody stopped what they were doing to stare, even Neddie in mid-lean. Nobody came into Mrs. Rodriguez's class late, so this was sure to be more interesting than anything in the copies of *History of New Mexico* that were tumbling from Neddie's arms.

Will nearly dropped his own stack of books. Slinking in the doorway were Rafael, Pablo, and Luis.

"Oh, no," Will muttered.

"Double oh, no," Neddie said, and dropped three more books.

"Who are those guys?" Kenichi whispered.

Will didn't have a chance to answer. Mrs. Rodriguez was sweeping the class with one of her killer stares. It was in a kid's best interest to hush up.

"Well, gentlemen," Mrs. Rodriguez said, pulling her square self out of her desk chair. Bracelets jingled and black hair swayed down her back as she approached the Three Amigos. "To what do we owe the honor of your presence—and late, I might add?"

Luis let a grunt escape through his always-chapped lips and jerked his head, which was still covered by a tweed golfer-style hat, toward Rafael. Will remembered that meant Rafael was going to do the talking.

Rafael's large blue eyes had always "stuck out" on his brown Hispanic face, but Will noticed as he started to talk that there was something different in them now. Where they'd once looked clueless and gullible, they now seemed hard and suspicious.

"We just got here," Rafael said. "This is s'posed to be our class."

"You have papers?" Mrs. Rodriguez said.

Rafael poked Pablo, which Will had seen him do more times than he cared to remember. Slender, light-haired Pablo dug his hand into the pocket of his baggy trousers and pulled out a fistful of papers. While Mrs. Rodriguez untangled them, the class buzzed. The Three Amigos surveyed the room, and Will surveyed *them*. They looked more changed than Will had realized on Saturday night.

Rafael was lankier, and he now had a scar on the side of his face. Pablo no longer looked shy and uncertain; he just looked as if he were ready to smack the first person who sneezed at him.

But it was Luis who had changed the most. It had always seemed to Will that Luis thought he could get away with anything because he was tough. Now, he didn't look as if he cared whether he got away with it or not. His eyes, sizing up the class through narrow slits, seemed to be daring anyone to question a move he might make.

It didn't appear to scare Mrs. Rodriguez any. She looked up from the papers and pointed a squared-off finger at three empty seats at the back of the room.

"Sit there for now, boys," she said.

They'd already slipped from "gentlemen" to "boys," but Will wanted to yell, *Don't let 'em sit in the back together! You're askin' for trouble!*

If there was any trouble, she was sure going to see it. As Will and Kenichi and Neddie finished passing out the books, she never took her eyes off of Luis and his friends.

"So who *are* these guys?" Kenichi whispered to Will as they slipped into their seats.

"Let's just put it this way," Will said. "I'd rather have Herb Vickers back in here than those three."

Kenichi's face went somber. They both knew what kind of trouble Herb Vickers had caused. It had been reason for celebration when his father had taken him out of Harrington Junior High and sent him back East to a private boarding school.

"All right, class," Mrs. Rodriguez said. "Today we're going to begin a unit on the history of Santa Fe. Now—"

The door opened again, and once again all eyes went in that direction. Will saw Luis take that opportunity to point a warning finger at him. It got Will's hackles up, but he forced himself to turn away.

The action at the door was less interesting this time. A short Hispanic boy was letting himself in, carrying a set of papers. These were unwrinkled as he handed them to Mrs. Rodriguez and said, "Excuse me, Señora. I had trouble finding the class-room."

The word "stupid" filtered up from the back of the room. Mrs. Rodriguez snapped her fingers, and all was quiet as she read the boy's papers.

He was definitely a different sort of Mexican-American from the Three Amigos, or even from Will's friend Juan-Carlos who had recently dropped out of school to help keep the family farm going until the men in his family could come home from the war. Luis, Pablo, Rafael, and Juan-Carlos all had Anglo blood, and they were rough and snarly.

This boy didn't appear to be Mexican at all, but maybe pure Spanish, with his glistening dark brown hair worn longer on top than most boys wore theirs and his dark-as-fudge eyes and cof-fee-with-milk-colored skin. He had a wide nose and a very full mouth, and his dense eyebrows came together as if he were con-centrating hard on Mrs. Rodriguez. In the few words he'd said, Will could tell he spoke English more correctly than the Three

Amigos could ever hope to, but he had a thicker accent, as if his first language were Spanish.

"His eyebrows are gonna tie together in a knot," Neddie whispered.

But just then Mrs. Rodriguez looked up from the papers at the boy and said, "Welcome to the class, Miguel." Slowly his frown melted into a smile that lit up his eyes and transformed him into someone different.

One of the girls whispered, "He's cute."

"He's a Percy pants," Rafael said from the back.

He was giving Pablo the usual poke—harder, Will saw, than it used to be—when Mrs. Rodriguez whipped her square face toward him and said, "There will be none of that here."

There was a long pause, during which Will didn't dare turn around to see the Amigos' reaction. When Mrs. Rodriguez seemed satisfied that she'd made her point, she turned back to the boy—Miguel—and said, "There's a seat there. Right behind Will Hutchinson. Will, raise your hand."

Will did. He was sure he heard snickering from the back, which he didn't doubt. Probably something to do with all the "Percy pants" belonging together.

Miguel looked down at the floor as he made his way to the seat behind Will, where Herb had once sat. His silky hair came forward and half covered his face, but he shook it back as he sat down, and Will could see the eyebrows knit together again. Next to him, Neddie was trying to achieve the same look with unsuccessful results.

"Please make our new students welcome, class, when you have the chance," Mrs. Rodriguez said.

Will turned around and nodded at Miguel. He didn't do the same for the Three Amigos. They could drop through the floor, and that would be fine.

"Now—if I can be allowed to do some teaching." Mrs.

Rodriguez swished her long hair over her shoulder and began her usual stroll around the room as she talked. "As you all probably know, Santa Fe was originally inhabited purely by what we now know as American Indians. We'll get back to the specifics later. During the 1600s—and that would be what century, class?"

"Seventeenth," Neddie said.

There was a light hissing from the back. Mrs. Rodriguez, if she heard it, ignored it. It made Will's hackles start up.

"Correct. That is when the Spanish came to the New World looking for gold."

"Smooth!" Rafael said.

Will could almost hear him and Pablo poking each other.

"Not quite," Mrs. Rodriguez said. "By the time Santa Fe was founded in 1610, it was obvious that there was no gold in New Mexico. So King Philip the Third of Spain decided to maintain it as a missionary field. They came looking for gold, and they left Christianity."

She paused and swept her eyes over the class, as if she expected someone to say something. Will put his hand up.

"That's good, isn't it?" he said.

"It was meant to be," Mrs. Rodriguez said. "The Indians on the pueblos, the Hopi in particular, were open to it at first. But starting in about the 1670s, the Spanish governors here tried to wipe out all traces of the Pueblo Indians' own religion. The Indians accepted the Catholic faith, but they wanted to practice it according to their traditional beliefs, and the governors weren't having it."

"Yeah, that's right!" came a voice from the back. Will was surprised that it was Luis. He usually made Rafael and Pablo do all the talking.

"If you have something to say, raise your hand," Mrs. Rodriguez said. "The Spanish were harsh with the Indians, there's no denying it. They prohibited the Indians from holding their own religious ceremonies so they had to have them hidden at night and underground."

Oh, Will thought, *that's why they have kivas.*

"The Spanish had three Pueblo shamans—that would be their medicine men—hanged for witchcraft, and that brought about the Pueblo Revolt of 1680 in which the Indians reclaimed Santa Fe."

"Boo!" said all Three Amigos.

"Hands," Mrs. Rodriguez said.

Will turned around. All three of them raised their hands and said, "Boo!"

"I can see we'll be having some private sessions after school to get you three up to speed on classroom behavior. In the meantime, you are not welcome to participate in the discussion. Now—"

"Hey—Teacher."

Will didn't even want to look this time. Mrs. Rodriguez was sure to explode. Nobody called her, "Hey—Teacher."

"You hafta let us talk," Luis said. "We hafta defend ourselves. You talkin' baloney 'bout our people. They great people."

"Let me say this first, and *then* I'll write out your referral to the office," Mrs. Rodriguez said. She was barely raising her voice, but her eyes were flashing. "Yes, the Spanish were a noble people at that time. I'm glad to defend that—I'm Hispanic myself. They did take this part of the country lawfully, with care, and with good conscience."

"Now you talkin'—"

"But those same 'great' people, the wealthy Spanish families of the seventeenth century, made Indians their slaves. They instructed them in the Catholic faith, and they promised them their freedom as soon as, in their judgment, the Indians were civilized enough to be able to handle it." Mrs. Rodriguez paused and gave the class, especially the back row, another look obviously designed to cook the misbehavior right out of them. "My question always is, who made them judge over what 'civilized' is?"

Will heard a desk scrape and turned around to see Luis standing right up on his chair.

"You not fit to be Spanish talkin' like that!" he said.

"And *you* are not fit to be in this classroom talking like *that*," Mrs. Rodriguez said. She turned to her desk and picked up her pen, but she quickly put it down and beckoned to Luis with her finger. "Never mind the paperwork. I'll take you down there myself. Class, read chapter six."

Every head went bookward as Mrs. Rodriguez took Luis by the arm and firmly escorted him out of the classroom. As soon as the door closed behind them, every head came back up, and the buzz started.

"Who *are* those guys?" Kenichi said to Will.

"Three of the most—"

But Will stopped as he felt a poke in his back. He half expected it to be Pablo and Rafael. It was little Miguel.

"Excuse me," he said, his voice soft and thick. It reminded Will of pudding. "Is it always like this in this class?"

"Are you kidding?" Neddie said. "This is phenomenal!"

Miguel's eyebrows twisted together.

"Don't worry about him," Will said. "He always uses big words."

"So do you, Anglo."

Will looked up. Rafael stood over him, his blue eyes cold and hard.

"You use a buncha big words, but you don' never say nothin'." He smiled a smile that didn't reach his eyes. "And pretty soon, everybody gonna know what a nothin' you are."

✢ ✤ ✢

Chapter Five

*N*obody said a word—in the whole class. Every ear seemed to be straining to hear what Rafael was saying to Will.

Except for Miguel's. He took both of his small, brown hands and placed them over *his* ears. When Rafael looked down at him, Miguel cut his eyes deliberately away and, as far as Will could tell, looked at nothing.

"You little lizard," Rafael said to him. Without even looking at Will again, he turned and went back to his desk.

At least they have somebody else to pick on now besides me, Will thought.

But he immediately felt bad, and he swiveled around in his chair toward Miguel.

"Don't pay any attention to Rafael and them," Will said.

"You'd better pay attention to them!" Neddie said. "If you don't watch your back—" He drew his hand across his throat, and Will and Kenichi rolled their eyes at each other. Neddie's imagination could be fun, but he could also get carried away with it.

Will grinned at Miguel. "I've never known any of them to actually slit anybody's throat. They just try to be tough, that's all."

"Huh," Neddie said.

Miguel bent his head toward the desk top. "Thank you," he said to Will.

Neddie was right about one thing, Will decided that afternoon as he was walking home from a rehearsal at the church for the youth Christmas pageant. You *did* have to be on your toes around the Amigos. He stole a look over his shoulder as he turned toward the Plaza—and then he rolled his eyes.

Wait a minute, he told himself. *All you gotta do is pray. Remember how you felt the other night when everybody was holding hands in the living room? You were* sure *God was there.* He straightened his shoulders. Nah. There was nothing to worry about.

The afternoon sun was turning the adobe buildings on the Plaza shades of gold and rose as Will crossed the Plaza. The air was that clear-cold that made him walk faster and lighter. But when he got to East San Francisco Street, he stopped. He wasn't sure, but he thought he saw Miguel about to go inside the LaFonda Hotel, dressed all in black. He appeared to be in a hurry because he disappeared quickly inside the front door.

Will felt a stab inside. The poor kid was probably still afraid Luis and those guys were going to come after him, and Will couldn't blame him. He himself had just been looking over his own shoulder not five minutes before.

Will glanced back at the oversized pocket watch on the corner. He didn't have to be home until five o'clock, so there was plenty of time. He crossed the street and went inside LaFonda.

It took a minute for his eyes to adjust to the light, because the lobby of the hotel was its usual warm-dark except for the fire crackling in the corner kiva. It wasn't a busy time—too early for supper or for the dancing that went on every night in the New Mexican Room. Any activity there was seemed to be coming from further back, where Will knew there was a big room for parties. None of the porters in their mariachi vests even seemed to notice him, so he crossed the tile floor and took a peek in the doorway of the south portal.

He pulled his head right back out. The entire long, windowed room was filled with tables of women in big hats and gloves. It was a cinch Miguel wasn't in *there*.

Will was just about to turn and run before they saw him and any cheek-pinching could commence, when one woman's shrill voice piped above the others: "Ladies, let me present my latest discovery—Miguel Otero!"

She can't mean the *Miguel*, Will thought. But the "Oh, how precious!" that rose in unison from the women made him look anyway.

There was Miguel, all right, dressed in shiny black pants and a matching vest thick with red embroidery, standing on a platform and holding a guitar.

"Jeepers," Will murmured to himself. "Who roped the poor kid into this?"

But Miguel didn't look as if he'd been hauled in, tied and gagged, at all. He made a rather elegant bow, swished back his silky dark hair, and smiled at his audience. Will had never heard so many gushy sighs at one time in his life. Miguel appeared to eat it all up like chocolate as he placed his hands on his guitar strings and began to play.

Will could feel his mouth dropping open. Miguel's right hand strummed the strings with the confidence of a pro, while his left hand fingered the frets with ease. The women were already fanning themselves and nudging each other. All Will could do was stand and stare—until Miguel finished his first piece. Then he knew he was clapping louder than any of them.

Will stayed in the doorway, hanging on every chord Miguel played the same way he soaked up a good radio show. He was listening to Miguel's fourth piece before it struck him that the boy hadn't hung his head to look at the floor one time. He had those women in the palm of his hand; that was obvious from the way they filled the hat he passed. Will dug into the pocket of his jacket and pulled out what was left of his week's allowance. As he was dropping it into the hat, pocket fuzz and all, he looked up to find Miguel watching him. A slow smile crossed his face, and he gave Will his own small bow.

Right after that, one of the porters began to cast dubious glances Will's way, so he decided he'd better leave. But all the way home, he didn't even think about the Three Amigos, much less check his back every now and then. His head was full of that kid Miguel, standing up there like he wasn't nervous at all. Considering the way he himself had felt that night on the stage with Dorothy Lamour, Will decided the kid was tougher than anybody thought.

Will was glad to see Mom's motorcycle in the driveway when he got home, and he burst through the back door ready to fill her and Fawn in on the whole thing. But when Mom looked up at him from the pot she was stirring on the stove, Miguel and everything else about the day drained out like Will's head was a sieve.

Mom's face was ash-gray, and the rims of her eyes were tell-tale red. There wasn't a twitch within a hundred miles. She was almost stone still.

Fawn, on the other hand, was crashing around the kitchen like a wild thing, dropping plates and silverware onto the table with a vengeance.

"What's going on?" Will said. "Did you guys have a fight?"

"No!" Fawn said, pelting the table with the salt and pepper

shakers. "I wish Uncle Al never told us about those rescued prisoners in the first place!"

"What's she talking about, Mom?" Will said.

"Your Uncle Al called," Mom said. "He got the list—"

"Yeah?"

Mom shook her head.

"Your dad's name wasn't on it," Fawn said. "Uncle Al just got everybody's hopes up for nothing!" She banged a glass onto the tabletop. "Now Mama Hutchie's all upset—"

"Fawn, of course I'm upset," Mom said. "I would much rather have gotten the news that Rudy was on his way home this very minute. But we didn't get news that he's been killed. He's still alive—we have to hang onto that." She looked at Will. "Are you all right, Son?"

Will's head was churning. *What happened, God? We prayed—don't You remember—we all prayed about this! I was sure You heard. I was sure You were gonna bring him home!*

"We're not going to give up," Mom said. "They just passed a bill that's going to guarantee money for college to men coming back from the war; and your dad *is* going to come back and get that and we *are* going to go on with our lives."

"How do you know?" Will said. He knew he was shouting at her, but he didn't know what else to do.

"I have faith," Mom said. "That's how I know."

"But it didn't do any good! I don't understand! I thought God heard us and He was gonna make everything okay! What's the use of prayin' if God doesn't listen?"

"Jeepers, Will, are you cryin'?" Fawn said. "You never cry—"

"I'm not cryin'!" Will said. "I'm not—"

They both just looked at him, Fawn shaking her head, Mom about to come over and stroke down his cowlick. Just then, he didn't want to be with either one of them.

"I gotta go," he said. And he pushed out the back door and ran out into the cold.

He could hear Fawn calling to him, but no one came after him as he tore down the driveway and crashed through the ice on the puddles on Canyon Road. Paseo de Peralta was slippery when he reached it, but he didn't slow down as he slipped and slid toward he-didn't-know-where, tears freezing on his face, sobs coming out in frosty puffs. He could barely see anything ahead of him—and that was okay. He didn't want to see or hear or think. He just wanted to run.

But even tearing past the adobes in the barrio of lonely DeVargas Street couldn't keep the thoughts from telling him *God didn't come through. You were so sure He would. You were so sure—*

The only thing that stopped the thoughts from writhing in his head was the sight, just across Old Santa Fe Trail, of three shadowy figures he'd seen so many times before, waiting for him in the dark. Then a clear thought came straight through: *If they see you crying, it'll be all over Harrington by morning.*

Not even slowing down, Will looked around for a place to hide. There was a stone wall in front of the San Miguel Mission. If he could stay in the shadows until he got to it, he might be able to leapfrog over it before they saw him.

But he knew the Three Amigos were bound to see him. They had a bird's-eye view from the corner where they were hanging out. Slowing down just enough to lean over, Will scooped up a handful of rocky dirt from the side of the road and pitched it toward the old narrow adobe house on the opposite corner. As he'd hoped, it made a racket as it splattered, and all three heads turned toward it. Praying that they'd look long enough to give him a chance to scramble up to the wall and drop himself over it, Will made a mad dash. Even as he hoisted his body over the side, he thought, *No. No more praying. I can't count on God.*

As he sank down behind the wall, he could hear Pablo and Rafael's arguing voices, but he couldn't make out what they were saying. Then Luis hushed them with a hiss, and Will heard nothing.

They're coming over here, I know they are, he thought. *I just hope they don't come behind this wall. Please, don't let them—*

Will bit on his hand to stop himself. He'd never realized how automatically he prayed.

He pressed his head against the wall to listen, but it was about two feet thick, and all he heard was his own pulse beating in his ear. Inching slowly upward, he peeked over the top. Pablo was still examining the house Will had thrown the dirt at. Rafael was on the corner just below the wall. Will lowered himself back down and looked behind him. There was a gate in front of the chapel that separated the wall at one point. Luis was leaning against it, his back to Will, looking lazily up and down the street.

He knows I'm in here, Will thought. *He's just waiting for me to try to get out.*

Will sagged against the wall. He didn't feel like fighting anybody right now. Not with tears and nose-gunk all over his face and this digging pain in his chest. Not just so he could get out of here and . . . do what? Go home? Where there was no Dad— where maybe there would *never* be Dad? Just to hear Mom talk about stuff like faith?

Will suddenly felt cold from the inside. Less than an hour before, he'd been filled with faith and hope. It was chilling to think it could all change so fast.

He looked toward the gate again. Luis had gotten very comfortable, arms folded, feet crossed. He was even whistling. Will's hackles came up, and he knew he was ready to make a move. Sizing up the shadows against the chapel, he flattened himself against the wall and crept along it, his back to the stones, his eyes on Luis.

Luis never moved, but continued to whistle as if it were only a matter of time before Will would try to get past him at the gate.

He actually thinks I'm stupid, Will thought.

Inching his way, Will finally came to the church itself. A wall of stone slanted out from the chapel just before the door, and Will stopped in its shadow and checked out Luis again. He was making some kind of signal to one of the other boys. It was definitely time to move.

Holding his breath and willing himself not to make a sound, Will slipped around the slanted piece of wall and melted into the shadow of the double doorway.

Please don't let the door—I mean, I hope the door doesn't creak.

He squeezed his eyes shut as he opened it, just wide enough to wriggle in. The wooden door was soundless, except for the soft sigh it made as it closed behind him. He waited, not breathing, but there were no footsteps clattering across the stones to get to him, no shouts of "He's in there!"

Just to be on the safe side, Will crept further into the church—and then he stopped and gasped. There were three people standing up at the front.

Will dove behind a straight-backed pew, heart pounding. The oak floor creaked under him and he clapped his hand over his mouth to keep from breathing too loudly. Only after he'd stayed that way until his legs ached from crouching did he crawl out from behind the pew bench and look again for the people.

They were still there, standing just as they'd been before, staring down at him. They didn't move—they didn't even seem to be breathing.

"They're not!" Will said out loud.

Then he clapped his hand over his mouth again, but his shoulders shook between laughing and crying. They weren't people. They were statues.

Will clung to one sleeve of his jacket with the other hand as he went slowly up the aisle, the floor creaking under him with every step. As he got closer, he realized the statue in the center was probably Jesus' mother, looking ghostly pale in a blue and white robe trimmed in gold gilt. Next to her was Jesus Himself, pointing to a gold heart-shaped necklace He was wearing.

I didn't know Jesus wore jewelry, Will thought.

The other statue he couldn't identify. It was some guy with a beard holding a baby with a dress on. Will knew a lot of Bible stories, but this didn't ring any bells.

Will was breathing more easily now, and he allowed himself to look around in the dark, shadowy chapel. It was chilly in there, but that wasn't all that made him shiver. It was all so unfamiliar, this church. There was an altar in the center up front, up against the wall. Behind it was a colorful set of shelves and curlicues, full of more small statues and paintings and portraits of people Will had no idea about.

Feels more like a museum than a church, he thought. *A* spooky *museum.*

There were more "exhibits" along the sides of the stone walls, walls so old there were weeds growing out of the cracks between them. Will saw a whole series of wood carvings, and from what he could figure out, they were all of Jesus on His way to be crucified. Will shivered and went on to the wall hangings, which appeared to be made of deerskin or buffalo hide. It was hard to tell what was painted on them, because the only light was coming from inside lampshades of hammered tin.

Will hugged his jacket around him and looked again at the colorful display behind the altar. It went all the way to the ceiling, and he let his eyes travel upward to the rough open beams which were nothing more than logs sawed in half lengthwise. They were so close together, Will was sure if he could have run a stick along them, they'd have played a rhythm, like running a stick along a picket fence—

His imaginary stick stopped running when his eyes got to the back of the church and collided with a narrow loft. There was a small group of men up there, on their knees, heads bowed over their long, loose-fitting brown robes.

Will kept looking long enough to decide these weren't statues, and made another dive for a spot between the end of a pew and the wall. No one came looking for him to boot him out, but Will wasn't relieved. This wasn't a friendly place, this church full of strange images and frightening figures and people in paintings he didn't recognize. Even the wall felt cold against his back, right through his jacket.

God doesn't seem close in here like He does at our church, Will thought. *He seems far away.*

Then it struck Will again—he wasn't going to pray anymore. It didn't do any good. Why did it matter if God was nearby or ten thousand miles from here?

The thought was lonelier than the church itself. Will could feel his throat tightening up again. He had to get out of there, Amigos or no Amigos.

He put his hand down on the floor to push himself up, but his palm came down on something soft and warm. Before he could jerk it away, another hand came around it. Another hand that held on tight.

✝ ✦ ✝

Chapter Six

*W*ill jerked away as if he'd been bitten by a rattler and in a spasm got to his feet.

"It's just me," said a soft voice below him.

Will squinted down at the floor and let the fear drain out of him. Two large brown eyes were looking up at him.

"Miguel!" Will said. "What in the Sam Hill are *you* doin' here? You about scared the pants off me!"

"Sorry," Miguel said. His smile had slowly spread across his face, but he glanced toward the loft and put his finger to his lips. "We should not disturb the monks."

"There's monkeys up there?" Will said as he sat down again on the floor next to Miguel.

Miguel shook his head. "No. Monks. They are the brothers of the church. They live here, take care of it—you know."

Will didn't but he nodded anyway. Presbyterians didn't have monks. "What are they doing up there?" he whispered.

"Praying. I think they are getting ready to practice."

"Practice what?"

"Chanting."

"Oh," Will said. He wasn't sure what chanting was, but he didn't want to appear too stupid in front of Miguel. "How come you know so much about this church?"

"I come to church here," Miguel said.

"You're a Catholic?"

Miguel knit his eyebrows together. "You do not like Catholics?"

"Sure, I guess I like them fine," Will said.

He looked around for something to change the subject to. He suddenly didn't want to leave after all, and talking to Miguel was already driving the cold aloneness away.

"If you are not a Catholic," Miguel said, "what are *you* doing in here?"

"Oh, well, I came in to—" Will's eyes caught on Miguel's large brown ones. The eyebrows were studiously scrunched together, as if he knew he would hear the absolute truth from Will and he wanted to get it all. "I was hiding from Luis and Pablo and Rafael. You know, the Three—"

"I know who you mean. I am hiding from them, too."

"No kiddin'!" Will said.

"Do not think I am a coward," Miguel went on.

"Oh, no, I don't."

"I just know when I cannot win."

Will felt himself grinning. "That's pretty smart."

"I try."

"So, why haven't I seen you around town before? How come you just came to Harrington today?"

"I only moved to Santa Fe last week. My mother and I came from Chimayo."

"How come?"

"We could not keep up our farm there—since my father left for the war."

"I know about that kind of stuff," Will said. "Everything got all turned upside down because of the stupid war."

Miguel nodded soberly. "My mother was never meant to be a farmer. Or I. It was falling down around us, so we came here to live with my Uncle José. He is a *santero*."

"A what?"

"*Santero*. You know, a person who makes statues of the saints."

"Oh, like those ones up there of Mary and Jesus and whoever that guy is."

"St. Anthony. Only, the ones Uncle José makes are not that big. They are the small ones people keep in their homes."

"Catholic people keep statues in their houses?" Will said. "Do they worship them or somethin', like idols?"

"No!" Miguel said. The eyebrows met again. "They are—how do I say it?—reminders. They remind us to pray, and sometimes we pray to a saint who has influence with God."

"What do you mean 'influence'?"

Miguel looked around. "You see the statue of St. Anthony there? If you had a problem with your marriage or are having a baby—"

"No, thank you!"

"You could pray through St. Anthony because he is the patron saint of marriage and childbirth."

"Even if I had a wife or kids—which I'm never gonna have—I wouldn't pray that way," Will said. "I learned you gotta go straight to God—you know, through Jesus, and nobody else. At least, that's what Pastor Bud and my mom told me—"

Will stopped. He could feel Miguel studying him.

"You do not believe it?" Miguel said.

"I don't believe in praying," Will said. "Not anymore. There's no point to it. I used to think God listened and gave you what you asked for if you really believed in Him, but I just found out it doesn't really work that way."

"Something bad happened."

It was a statement, not a question, but almost before he realized it, Will found himself telling Miguel about Dad and the prison camp and the news from Uncle Al—everything. When he finally wound down, he looked sheepishly at Miguel.

"Sorry. I didn't mean to go blubbering about all that stuff."

But Miguel shook his head, eyebrows firmly pinched together. "My heart hurts for you," he said.

Will tried to smile. "You're kiddin', right?"

"No," Miguel said. "I would not kid about that."

Will felt the tears threatening again, so he said quickly, "You sure speak English good. Better than Luis and them." He gave a shot laugh. "Better than me. You talk all proper—which is good. I mean, you don't sound uppity, you just sound—I don't know, you just sound correct or something."

"That is my mother. She taught me when I was a baby, and she does not let me make a mistake."

"That's for sure."

They were quiet for a minute, and in the silence the monks above them began to sing—only it wasn't like any singing Will had ever heard. The words were in some other language, and most of the notes were the same. But the sound echoed through the church and made it somehow friendlier.

"Is that chanting?" Will said.

Miguel smiled and nodded. He had his head leaned against the wall, eyes closed, as if that helped him hear the music better.

"You really like music, huh?" Will said. "By the way, you sure play the guitar swell. I heard you today."

"I saw you there," Miguel said. "Thank you for putting money in my hat. I will return the favor someday."

"You don't hafta," Will said. "I wanted to do it. I never heard a kid play like that before."

In fact, Will thought, he'd never met a kid who was like Miguel in any way. He was small, but he wasn't puny like Neddie. He was strong, but he wasn't tough like Luis. He was serious, but he wasn't bitter like Kenichi could sometimes be.

And he seems like he's happy—not all tied up in knots inside like I am.

Maybe that was why he wanted to sit there longer and talk to Miguel and listen to the monks chanting from the loft. But he knew by now Mom would think he'd had enough time to cool off and would expect him home.

"What time do you have to be home?" Will said.

"Before the bell rings."

"What bell?"

Miguel pointed to the ceiling. "The San José bell—up in the tower. It rings at eight o'clock. I have to be home before then."

"I wonder if Luis and those fellas are still outside," Will said.

"I do not think their parents give them a time to be home," Miguel said.

"No, but I bet the police do. 'Course, that never stopped them before." Will nudged Miguel. "Let's go out together. Maybe that way at least one of us can get away."

"I can run fast," Miguel said. "I will lead them one way, and you go home the other."

"Deal," Will said.

But when they closed the door on the chanting of the monks, there wasn't a sign of Luis or Pablo or Rafael. After checking every shadowy nook and cranny, they were satisfied that the coast was clear, and they said good-bye at the gate.

"See you tomorrow," Miguel said. "I do not think school will be so bad now."

Will nodded, but as he turned and trudged toward home, he

wasn't quite so sure about that. Out here, with the ice clinging to the coyote fences and the moonlight hitting hard against the adobe walls, what he was going to face when he got to his house slammed into him again. Fawn being angry. Mom being hopeful.

And he was right. Fawn was pouting over her homework at the kitchen table, and Mom was in the living room, hanging balls on the Christmas tree.

"What do you think, Will?" she said. "Is it shaping up?"

"I guess so."

"I'm also thinking of getting a carved Nativity scene, too—what do they call them here—*nacimiento?*"

"Sure."

"I made some *bischochitos* you can dip in cocoa. I think just this once you can have dessert for dinner."

Mom turned as if to catch his smile, but Will didn't give her one. She set the box of ornaments down and came toward him. He stuffed his hands in his pockets and looked at the floor. She didn't try to pull them out.

"I know you're disappointed," she said. "We all are—probably your dad most of all. But I'm not giving up. He wouldn't want that, especially from you."

"Who says I'm giving up?" Will said.

"You did."

"When?"

"When you said there was no use in praying anymore."

Will shuffled a few steps backward, eyes still on the floor. "Just because I'm not gonna pray doesn't mean I'm giving up. There's still stuff I can do."

Mom took hold of his chin and jerked his face up to hers. Will was too surprised to pull away.

"You can't do much without God, Will, I'll tell you that. Please don't—"

The phone rang in the kitchen. As Mom loosened her grip on

his chin, Will turned away and bolted for it. Still clinging inside his head was the thought: *It could be Uncle Al. He could have made a mistake. I'd even forgive him—*

But it was Bud on the other end of the line.

"Hey, Will!" he said. "Listen, I wonder if you could do something for me—well, for the whole church, actually."

Will's hackles prickled. "I don't know," he said.

There was a pause no longer than a second, but when Bud went on, his voice was a little more careful. "It turns out the part of Joseph in the pageant is going to be a little too much for Abe. We all knew that, but you kids wanted him to have the part—"

Bud paused as if he expected Will to say something, but he didn't. His tongue was ready to lash out—at anybody—and he didn't want it to be Bud.

"I talked to him about it," Bud went on, "and he agrees with me, and of course when I asked him who he thought should take his place, he said 'Will'—"

"No," Will said.

"You could trade parts with him. You won't hurt his feelings. Abe wants you to do it. He's already dragged out the costume so Tina can alter it—"

"No," Will said again.

Bud gave a cautious chuckle. "You sound pretty certain about that. You sure you don't want to at least sleep on it before you decide?"

Once more, Will said, "No."

There was no chuckle this time. "May I ask why?"

Another "no" was on the tip of Will's tongue, but his hackles were standing all the way up by that time, and he couldn't hold back what he really wanted to say.

"Because if God isn't going to do anything for me," Will said, "then I don't see why I should do anything for Him. Matter of fact, I don't want to be in the pageant at all. You can give my part to somebody else."

In the stunned silence that followed, Will added, "I gotta go do homework. Bye."

It was two days before Will talked to Kenichi or Neddie or Abe about Uncle Al's call. They knew already, but Will didn't even want to think about it, much less discuss it. It was a fact now—done—over with. No point in going back to it.

But after two days, Neddie couldn't leave it alone anymore. On Friday, the last day of school before Christmas vacation, he leaned across the cafeteria table at lunch and said, "Are you gonna be sulky for the rest of your life, Will? Are you gonna be a sulky teenager, driving around with your chin on the steering wheel? Then go to college and sulk in your football helmet like this—" He stuck out his lower lip like a sofa. "And then are you gonna be a sulky father who—"

"Knock it off, Neddie," Will said—sulkily.

"He's kinda got a point, Will," Kenichi said. "There's stuff I need to talk to you about, but you've been in such a bad mood, nobody can talk to you about anything."

"It is difficult when your father is in the war," Miguel said.

"Don't I know it?" Kenichi said, his cheeks going blotchy. "I got a father over there too—so do you—so does just about everybody—"

"All right, all right," Will said. "So what did you want to talk to me about? I won't be in a bad mood."

Kenichi pressed his lips together for a minute. Then he said, "Neddie, do you and Miguel mind—could I talk to Will in private?"

Neddie and Miguel disappeared without an argument. Will watched them go, and he felt his eyes narrow.

"Do they already know what you're gonna talk to me about?" he said.

"Yeah," Kenichi said. "*They* weren't in a bad mood, so I told them."

"Okay, so you told them what?" Will's mouth was going dry, and he wanted to run. Any more bad news, and he wasn't sure he could keep from punching something.

"You know Yoji's going to college in Albuquerque in January," Kenichi said.

"Yeah."

"And you know how he promised my father he wouldn't leave my mom and Emi and me."

"Yeah—hey, you mean Yoji's *not* going to college, after all the money we raised for his scholarship?"

"Keep your shirt on. He's going. But we're going with him—the whole family."

Will sagged so far he hit bottom. "You're moving to Albuquerque?"

Kenichi nodded. "Right after Christmas. My mom got a job down there and everything—a good job. We can get a bigger apartment—"

"But you're my best friend," Will said.

Kenichi nodded and looked away. Will couldn't look at him either. They were sitting in silence, staring at opposite walls, when Miguel and Neddie came back.

"Did he tell you?" Neddie said.

Will nodded. *Go away, Neddie,* he thought. *Or I'm gonna say something dumb to you.*

"Doesn't it stink?" Neddie said. "Don't you just want to build this huge roadblock in the middle of the highway so they can't go? Don't you want to drop a big wrecking ball on top of his mom's car—"

"No, Neddie," Will said between clenched teeth. "But I'm gonna drop one on you if you don't shut up."

Neddie looked as if he'd been stung.

"You didn't have to say that, Will," Kenichi said.

"No worries," Miguel said. He put a hand on Neddie's arm. "He is just upset."

"Well, looky at what the sissy is doing now."

All four of their heads jerked up. Luis was standing right behind Miguel, with Pablo and Rafael on either side of him. Every one of them looked as if his smile had been gashed into his face with a knife.

Miguel moved his hand away from Neddie's arm. Neddie stared at the spot as if there just might be cooties there.

"Hey," Will said. "Miguel's no sissy."

"He no sissy?" Luis said. He clutched the front of his shirt in mock amazement. The students in the cafeteria turned to watch the action.

"You don't know he is a sissy gee-tar player?" Luis said.

"Yeah—he wears a fancy suit to play gee-tar for the ladies!" Rafael added.

He and Pablo exchanged pokes as Rafael went on. "He passes his bonnet and they all give him money—what do you buy with it, Mee-Guel? More fancy clothes? Dollies?"

The cafeteria was by now in an uproar. Everyone was either hooting with laughter or discussing the matter, and half the boys were climbing on top of the tables to get a better view.

"So he plays the guitar, Luis," Will said, staring angrily at the table top. "That doesn't make him a sissy."

"But he will run if we chase him—won't you—sissy?"

Luis raised a hand and snapped his fingers. Almost before his fingers had separated, Pablo and Rafael had Miguel on his feet. Luis put his hand in the center of Miguel's back and gave him a shove.

"Run, sissy!" he said. "Run like a rabbit!"

Whether Miguel would have, no one ever found out. For just as he stumbled forward at Rafael's push, Will leapt from his seat and snatched Luis by the back of the shirt.

"Leave him alone!" Will shouted. "Leave him alone or I'll kick your tail!"

In the moment it took Luis to recover from his shock, Will knocked him backwards with the heels of his hands, and he dropped to the floor.

"Get him, Will!" somebody yelled.

Will jumped on top of Luis and grabbed him by the hair. Luis, it turned out, was much stronger than the last time Will had tussled with him, and he rolled over and laid Will flat on his back. Will looked over Luis's shoulder to watch his own fists pound the Spanish boy's back, but both of his hands froze in mid-punch.

Mrs. Rodriguez was standing over them.

✝ ⚜ ✝

Chapter Seven

*B*reak it up, both of you!" Mrs. Rodriguez said. Her voice was sharp, and her square jaw was set in anger. "Come on, on your feet!"

Will was more than anxious to obey, but Luis was heavy on top of him, and he didn't budge. At least, not until Mrs. Rodriguez reached down and grabbed the back of his shirt and yanked him to a standing position. Luis looked surprised for a moment before he drew his face back into its usual sullen expression.

The minute Luis was up, Will scrambled to his feet. The whole cafeteria had fallen into that kind of silence that comes when people are licking their chops to witness the worst. Will searched for a pair of friendly eyes. Neddie wouldn't look at him. Kenichi was shaking his head in disgust. Only Miguel met his gaze; he looked as if he were about to watch a beheading.

Will swallowed hard, and his heart was definitely racing, but the hackles were still standing up on the back of his neck. *Just let me hit him one time, Mrs. Rodriguez,* he thought. *Just one time, and I'll feel better.*

It was obvious, though, that there was to be no more hitting. Mrs. Rodriguez had Luis by the arm with one hand and Rafael by the back of his collar with the other, steering them toward the door. Pablo was trailing behind, as if to separate himself from his two amigos was out of the question.

"Coach Piña!" Mrs. Rodriguez called to the wizened man who was just hurrying into the cafeteria with his whistle in his mouth. "Take these three down to see Mr. Tarantino. Fighting— again."

"He started it!" Rafael said, trying to get around Mrs. Rodriguez to point at Will.

"Tell it to Mr. T.," Mrs. Rodriguez said.

Coach Pina got them all in tow, Rafael still complaining at the top of his lungs, Luis muttering under his breath. Even in his rattled state, Will thought it was a good thing Coach Pina was hard of hearing.

"All right, people, back to your business," Mrs. Rodriguez said to the still-drooling crowd. "It's all over."

Most of the boys gave a disappointed groan which Mrs. Rodriguez ignored as she cupped her square hand around Will's arm and led him off toward the small room off the cafeteria where the teachers ate. There was a window in it through which the teachers on duty could keep an eye on the students. Will hadn't been thinking about that when he'd shoved Luis to the floor. He hadn't been thinking about anything but hitting some- body.

"Have a seat," Mrs. Rodriguez said, closing the door behind her.

"I'd rather stand, if that's okay," Will said.

"It is not okay. Sit."

Will did, hackles prickling anew.

"Now, do you want to tell me what that was all about?" she said.

"No," Will said.

Mrs. Rodriguez's eyebrows went up like two flat box tops. "No?" she said. "I thought you and I were beyond that."

"I just don't wanna talk about it," Will said.

"You're going to have to talk about it to somebody—it doesn't have to be me."

"Why?" Will said. "It isn't gonna change anything."

"What is this I'm seeing?" Mrs. Rodriguez said. "What's gotten into you lately? You have a chip on your shoulder so big it's going to take a crane to pick it off."

"Maybe I don't want it picked off," Will said. The words flew from him like rocks out of a slingshot, and he couldn't stop them. He wasn't even sure he wanted to.

"If it doesn't come off, you're going to be in a lot more trouble than just a fight in the cafeteria."

"That wouldn't even of happened if everybody would just leave people alone."

"Ah." Mrs. Rodriguez's face softened. "I thought I was right. You were defending Miguel, weren't you?"

"I guess."

Mrs. Rodriguez folded her square hands on the tabletop. "Look, Will, I asked the class to be nice to him. I didn't expect you to go several rounds with the school bully for him. Can't you find some other way to 'welcome' Miguel?"

Will pulled back the slingshot, but he didn't let it go this time. It would have been too much to say, *You know what I said about people leaving people alone? I wish you'd do it. I wish you'd leave me alone and let me do things my own way. I don't need your help. I can't count on anybody anyway—not even God. Especially God!*

He looked up to see Mrs. Rodriguez looking back at him so

hard and so square, he thought for a moment he'd actually said it out loud. She gave a sharp nod.

"All right. I was going to try to work this out with you on my own, but I can see I'm not the person to handle it. I'm sending you to Mr. Tarantino—both for fighting and for that big boulder on your shoulder that's *making* you fight. Do I need to walk you down, or can I trust you to get there on your own?"

"I'll go by myself," Will said. *'Cause that's what I want. I just wanna be left alone.*

The cafeteria was empty when he walked through it, and the halls echoed vacantly as he made his way to Mr. T.'s office. *Yeah, by myself,* he thought. *That's where I wanna be.*

Mr. T.'s secretary was at lunch. It felt strange to flop down in a chair in her outer office instead of checking her desk for a list of jobs to do. For the first few months of school, before he'd found Neddie and before Kenichi had come, Will worked in Mr. T.'s office during lunch, ushering in kids in trouble for a talking-to. Now he was one of those kids.

He slouched back in the chair and swung his legs, arms folded across his chest. Yeah. By himself. He could think his own thoughts. Do things his own way.

The clock above the secretary's desk ticked loudly. That was the only sound in the room. Inside his head, however, it began to get noisy.

It isn't bad enough Dad wasn't rescued. Now Kenichi's moving away. I hurt Neddie's feelings. Miguel thinks I'm some bully because I jumped Luis. Luis and those guys'll have it in for me even more now. God, what am I supposed to do—

God? Will shook his head at the empty room. No. No Godtalk. That didn't do any good. All it did was get people's hopes up. Bud and Mom were just trying to make him feel better.

And he didn't.

When the inner office door opened, Will was relieved to have something to distract him, even if it *was* Rafael, Luis, and Pablo, heading for the outer door.

"That's it," Mr. T. said behind them. "Look to neither left nor right. Just go straight to class. I will see all three of you here after school."

Rafael and Pablo shrugged like they were trying to get a cat off their backs as they made their exit. Luis paused in the doorway and slanted a sneer at Will.

"Watch it," Mr. T. said, warning tone in gear.

Luis left and let the door slam behind him.

"Mr. T.," Will said, "you're gonna have to do something worse than keep them after school. They've been in reform school, and it didn't even change them."

Mr. T., who was wearing his usual Western-style shirt and string tie and cowboy boots, squinted at Will out of his tanned-leather face. Will always thought he looked as if he should be out rustling cattle, but right now he was the principal, and Will could feel him making a principal's decision. For the first time since he hit Luis, Will began to squirm.

"Suppose you let me worry about those boys and you worry about this one." He tapped Will on the shoulder. "Come on in."

Will followed him into the inner office he had come to love and straddled one of the chairs made out of a saddle. Mr. T. straddled the other one.

"I don't need to worry about me," Will said. "I'm fine. I'm figurin' a lot of things out."

"Oh?" Mr. T. said. One white eyebrow that matched his hair shot up. "You're figuring out that picking a fight with a tough guy like Luis is your best bet?"

"He made me mad!" Will said. "He was pickin' at Miguel, and I got sick of it. People need to leave other people alone."

"If you think I'm going to leave you alone, Will, you have

another think coming. Now just settle down and tell me what happened."

"It isn't gonna happen again, Mr. T.—"

"Talk."

Will did. It was hard at first, because he still didn't want to. His head was still screaming, *Leave me alone! Let me do this my own way!* But the more he talked and the more Mr. T. nodded his snowy head and quietly fingered his string tie, the quieter the screaming got. By the time Will was finished, there was a tiny flicker of hope about the size of a birthday candle flame. Maybe Mr. T. *could* help him the way nobody else could.

"I will commend you for one thing, Will," Mr. T. said.

"What's 'commend'?" Will said. "Is that good?"

"It's like a pat on the back. I commend you for wanting to stick up for Miguel. He's new. He's unique. You of all people know what that's like."

"See—that's all I was doin'—just standin' up for him."

"That's the other side of it, though, Will," Mr. T. said. "That wasn't 'all' you were doing."

"Yes, it was!"

"Will." Mr. T. leaned forward on his saddle. "I know about the news about your father. And I know Kenichi's moving away. Those are two big things you have to wrestle with right now. But it's those things you need to wrestle with—not the other boys."

Mr. T.'s eyes squinted in a friendly way, but Will suddenly didn't feel like he needed a friend. The tiny candle flame went out, and his neck started to prickle again.

"There's nothing to wrestle with," Will said. "From now on, I won't count on anybody, that's all."

"I hate to see you take that attitude," Mr. T. said.

"What attitude am I supposed to take? Everything is all messed up—"

"It seems that way right now. That's why we go to God—all

of us—your mother, Pastor Bud, me. I can tell you that praying for Luis and his friends makes a lot more sense than going at it with them in the school cafeteria."

Will shook his head. The hackles were standing straight up. "Praying doesn't do any good," he said. "If I'm gonna do something, I'm gonna do it my own way from now on."

Mr. T. squinted at him for what seemed like a long time. Then he leaned forward again, elbows resting on his knees, so that his face was close to Will's. When he spoke, it was in a voice Will knew he saved for the worst cases. It was his cattle-prodding voice.

"You can try your 'own way,' Will, but I'll guarantee you it's going to get you nowhere. I believe in letting boys find that out on their own—within limits."

Will forced himself not to look down. "What limits?" he said.

"You will follow the rules of this school or face the consequences, just like everyone else. You will respect the judgment of the people in authority here. You will refrain from taking out your anger and your fear and your frustration on other people while you are in this building. Am I clear?"

For the smallest part of a second, Will wanted to say, *Yes! And I'm sorry! Would you help me?*

But what if Mr. T. couldn't? What if nobody could? Wouldn't it just hurt more?

The second passed, and Will lifted his chin. "You're clear," he said. "What's my punishment?"

"It's this: Don't come back to this office until you're ready to be the real Will Hutchinson. And that means you'd better not give anyone reason to send you down here until that time."

Will felt as if he'd been shot. He wanted to sag, but it was too late. "Okay," he said. "Can I go now?"

Mr. T. nodded. Will could feel him watching him all the way to the door.

"Have a nice Christmas, Will," he said.

"Yeah," Will said. But he didn't turn around.

It had never seemed less like Christmas to Will. He and Mom had spent three other Christmases without Dad, but somehow they'd always managed to make the season merry with presents and bischochitos and rides to look at the farolitos lit all over town. This year, Will changed the channel on the radio every time "White Christmas" came on. He just wished Christmas would go by without him.

There was no chance of that. That Sunday was the Christmas pageant, and although Will had decided not to be in it, Mom made him go and at least support Fawn and Abe and Kenichi and Emiko.

He watched glumly from the balcony of the church as the other kids acted out the Nativity scene below. Abe was a frightened, reluctant Joseph—until he began to sing. Even Will stirred in his third-row balcony seat as Abe filled the church with a voice like a boy-angel's.

"I didn't know he could sing like that," Mom whispered to Will.

Nor did they know that Fawn had acting talent. At one point in the play, a party of Indians, led by a convincingly reverent Fawn, entered the scene and got on their knees before the Baby Jesus.

"Who are these strangers come to attend the birth of the Infant Savior?" said a timid Emiko-playing-Mary.

Fawn stood up out of her group and with spirit in her voice said, "We, too, are people for whom the Son of God was born on earth, that He might save us."

A gentle murmur went through the church, especially among the American Indians in the pews. Mom leaned into Will again.

"I'm surprised Bud got Fawn to play an Indian role," she

whispered. "But she's doing it so well. Look how loved-by-God all the Indians in the audience look."

Will had to admit Fawn was pretty convincing. It almost made him think a kind thought about God.

But then he turned from the scene and looked out the window at the snow on the Jemez Mountains. What good did it do to feel loved by God? Things were lousy anyway.

In spite of the preparations over the next few days, that feeling didn't change in Will. He went through the motions of wrapping his presents for Fawn and Mom in the Sunday funny papers and dunking bischochitos in hot cocoa and carrying the turkey home from Roybal's for Mom to roast for Christmas Eve dinner. But nothing sent the shivers of anticipation through him the way other Christmases had. Not even the two things that had everybody else practically doing a dance.

One was that Uncle Al called—not with more news of Dad, but to announce that he would be arriving Christmas morning to spend a day or two with them.

"I don't want to see him," Will said to Fawn while Mom was still squealing with him on the phone.

"Uncle Al's swell!" Fawn said. "And he always brings chocolate!"

"He also always brings bad news," Will said.

Fawn held her cookie in mid-dunk and frowned at Will. "I was mad at him at first, too, but at least he didn't say your dad was, you know, not *ever* comin' home. I don't get you."

"You would if it was your dad," Will said. "All the news you get about your dad is good."

He was right. That afternoon, the second piece of excitement arrived—a package for Fawn from her father, postmarked France.

The Hutchinsons always opened their presents Christmas morning, but Mom didn't make her wait until the next day. Fawn tore into the brown wrapper and pulled out a present each for Mom and Will and two more boxes. One was a pair of boots— Anglo boots, Fawn was quick to point out—that fit her just right and were going to be perfect in the snow that was coming down like thick balls of cotton outside their windows.

The other package was big and took both Fawn and Mom to open. With the paper torn away, something white billowed out over the edge of the box and left them all staring, puzzled. Will stopped examining the toy airplane Fawn's father had sent him and touched the white fabric.

"This feels like what they make parachutes out of," Will said. "Uncle Al sent me that toy one—"

"It *is* a parachute!" Mom said. "Look, this must be where the lines were attached."

"We can have some fun with this, Will!" Fawn said. "We could put on our own strings and jump off the roof—"

"Before you go plunging to your deaths," Mom said, "maybe you'd better read your dad's letter. I'm thinking there's an explanation in here."

With eager fingers, Fawn unfolded the several-page letter Mom handed her. Will felt suddenly uneasy. His hackles were itching, and his thoughts stirred like irritable old men being awakened from their naps.

How come she *gets a letter from her father? How come I don't? This isn't fair—*

But the thoughts made him squirm, and he smacked them aside and tried to focus on Fawn. She was looking wide-eyed at the handwriting with its censored blot-outs, and Will was sure he saw her hands shaking.

"Would you read it, Mama Hutchie?" Fawn said. "I don't read that good yet."

"Sure," Mom said. "But just for the record, Fawn, you read just fine."

"So go on," Fawn said. "Start from the beginning."

Mom settled in next to the fire and Fawn sat at her feet, watching her lips as if she could see the words coming out. Will sat on the window seat, where they wouldn't be looking at him.

Dear Fawn, (Mom read)

Merry Christmas! I hope this reaches you before the big day. I know how slow the mails can be, so I'm sending this to you in August. Even if you don't get it until after Christmas, I know God will let you know that I'm thinking of you.

"Wait a minute," Fawn said. "Are you sure you read that right? My dad doesn't ever talk about God."

"That's what it says," Mom said. Her lips twitched. "You think some impostor wrote it?"

"No. Go on," Fawn said, and took up her lip-watch again.

I'm sure you're wondering why I've sent you a parachute. Believe me, it took some doing, because it's government property, but I pulled some strings. This is the parachute that brought me safely to earth from the plane on D-day. It kept me hanging in a tree, radio gear and all, until one of our men came along to cut me down. I would like for you to see that this parachute is made into a wedding dress for he-mah, your mother. You may need to ask Mrs. Hutchinson to help you, but I want it to be a surprise. When I come home, I want your mother and me to be married in a church, so that our union is made before God. You know that it is against Indian law for a Tanoan like your mother to marry a Navajo like myself, so neither of our tribes recognize that we are husband and wife. But since I have been over here, Fawn, I have come to know our Lord Jesus Christ, and I know that any marriage blessed by Him is a true marriage. Indians from many different tribes are fighting side by side over here, and all of us are working with the belegaana, you know, the white men. The differences that once existed among us have faded beneath the need for all of us, belegaana *included, to act as one nation.*

However, I have also learned here that it is important to know who you are. I know that you have been welcomed into the Hutchinson house as if you were one of their own, and there is no end to my gratitude for that, especially where it comes to your education. I have learned how important that is. But I want you to remember that you are an American Indian. You are one who lives very well among white people, and I am glad for that. I think there will be much you can teach me when I come home. But please learn as much as you can about where you have come from, too. You have my blessing to spend time on San Ildefonso Pueblo, even though it is Tanoan and not my tribe. You can be the link that brings your mother's family to-gether with me, so that we can live at peace as a family.

I love you, and I promise you that as soon as we have forced the Germans into unconditional surrender, I will be home. Until then, pray every day and let our Lord Jesus Christ be your guide.

Shush

"Shush?" Mom said. The word came shakily from Mom's lips as she handed the letter back to Fawn. Will could see the tears glistening in her eyes. He swallowed his own back.

"That's his Navajo name," Fawn said. "It means 'bear.' "

"Well, that's the best Christmas present anyone could ever receive," Mom said. "I'm so happy for you, Fawn."

Mom looked over at Will, and he knew she was expecting him to say something. He chewed on his lip. The only words that sprang to his mind were, *What about my dad? What about our family? Where is 'our Lord Jesus Christ' for us?*

Will couldn't force these thoughts to go away, and his disappointment washed over him once again.

✝ ◦✝◦ ✝

Chapter Eight

*I*t was snowing hard the next day when Uncle Al finally arrived. He'd managed to get a ride to Santa Fe from the train station in Lamy, but the roads were piled high with snow, and it was nearly noon by the time he knocked on their front door. Mom was the first one there. Will stayed put on the window seat and pretended to be checking out his new chemistry set.

"Merry Christmas, Miss Rudolpho!" Uncle Al said. "And there's that Little Doll!"

Fawn wrinkled her nose at him, but she didn't protest as Uncle Al scooped her up. There was no use in fighting Uncle Al once he'd come up with a nickname.

"Where's my nephew?" he said.

Will barely looked up from his chemistry set, but it was long enough to see the instructions in Mom's eyes: Get up and greet your uncle, and don't be rude.

"Hello, sir," Will said, and he stood up and put out his hand.

"We're being formal, are we?" Uncle Al said. "You have a lot of class, Willie Boy—just like your old man." He grinned at Mom and said quickly, "I mean, your father. Your mother doesn't like it when I expose you kids to bad habits from my old neighborhood."

"If that's the worst you teach them, I'll be grateful," Mom said.

She put her elbow on Uncle Al's broad shoulder—Uncle Al was a good head shorter than she was—and grinned into his dark, snappy eyes. He grinned back, a sort of lopsided tough guy smile that had always made Will like him before.

But I don't like him that much anymore, Will reminded himself. *I can't count on him.*

"You hungry?" Mom said. "We have turkey and trimmings left over from last night."

"I'm starving. I could eat the Little Doll here." He picked up Fawn again and pretended to bite into her arm. She punched at him playfully. Will felt a longing he had to push away.

"But I think I should take you out for dinner," Uncle Al said. "How about that inn? That real Spanish place downtown?"

"LaFonda?" Mom said. "It's expensive, Al. Dinners are two dollars and up, and I don't know how much traditional Christmas fare there will be."

"Don't you worry about the dough, Miss Rudolpho," Uncle Al said. "And as for tradition, I don't think this is your average traditional Christmas anyway, eh, Willie Boy?"

Will started to shrug, but the look in Uncle Al's eye stopped him before he could even get his shoulders lifted. The black eyes, looking into him from beneath the shock of dark hair that spilled out over his forehead, seemed suddenly old and wise. Will wanted to nod his head, and maybe even throw his arms around Uncle Al's neck, or perhaps shove him to the floor and wrestle it out with him. But he couldn't do any of those things—not without going back on his own word. *I'm gonna do things my own way from now on. You can't count on anybody. Especially God.*

Uncle Al didn't wait for an answer but instead hurried everybody into coats and boots and mufflers and gloves, and linked arms with Mom as they led the way through a foot of flakes toward LaFonda.

"I'm not takin' your arm," Fawn said to Will. "So don't even think about it or I'll give you a snow sandwich."

"Okay," Will said.

"Oh," Fawn said.

She stuffed her hands into the pockets of her coat and suddenly looked a little lonely. Will felt a stab.

"Nice boots," he said.

"Isn't my dad the best?" she said.

The stab went away, and the hackles came up again. Will kept his mouth shut the rest of the way.

The Plaza was under a blanket of snow, untrodden by feet. The amount of piñon smoke chugging out of chimneys told them most people were snug in their homes.

The people who *had* been hearty enough to brave the weather all seemed to be inside LaFonda, gathered around tables set up in La Cantina, which was the cocktail room, the New Mexican Room, and even the south portal. There was a Christmas tree in the lobby, and the air was delicious with the aromas of pumpkin and mince pies, turkey, and cranberry sauce.

"Smells pretty traditional to me," Uncle Al said. "Where shall we sit?"

"I hear music from back there," Mom said, pointing to the south portal. "Let's try that."

Will knew even before they got to the doorway whose music it was. Miguel was sitting on his platform with his guitar, dressed in his black costume with a sprig of holly pinned to his vest.

"That kid has to work on Christmas?" Fawn said as they seated themselves at a table near the evergreen-festooned windows.

"He doesn't look like he's working too hard," Mom said. "Look at the expression on his face. Pure contentment."

"I bet he doesn't have a father away in the war, eh, Willie Boy?"

Will looked quickly at Uncle Al. He was giving him that I-know-what-you're-thinking eye, and his mouth read: *I'm not going to leave you alone until you talk to me, Willie Boy.*

"His father *is* away in the war," Will said.

"You know him?" Mom said.

Fawn poked Will in the side. "Who is he? How come I don't know him?"

"He's in my class at school," Will said. "He's new."

"He certainly plays beautifully," Mom said.

Will had to agree with that while the Hutchinsons stuffed themselves with Christmas dinner and listened to Miguel's music. Even more than before, Miguel seemed to be connected to his guitar as he coaxed it to sing "Silent Night." Uncle Al had to break out his handkerchief to wipe his eyes.

"The boy just looks so peaceful," Mom said.

I don't see how he can be, Will thought. He tried to get his anger going to protect him from his own tears that threatened to come, but he couldn't stir the irritation up. He could only feel the sadness, and he wanted to be peaceful like Miguel.

Miguel livened up the music after that, and the Hutchinson party sang while they finished up their pie. Even Will joined in, mostly to keep himself from crying. When he took his break, Miguel came over to their table and kissed Mom's and Fawn's hands and then smiled his slow smile at Will.

"Merry Christmas, my friend," he said. "You are better?"

"Better than what?" Fawn said, secretly wiping her hand off on her skirt where Miguel couldn't see.

"Better than ever!" Uncle Al said. He raised his punch glass. "A toast to my nephew, William Hutchinson, and to his young friends. Friends are a treasure. May you always cherish each other."

They all clinked glasses—and Uncle Al and Will clinked glances. Will wasn't surprised when, as the four of them walked home the long way so they could see the 800 farolitos at the big Victorian mansion on Paseo de la Cuma, Uncle Al put his arm around Will's shoulders and steered him out of earshot of Mom and Fawn.

"Better than *what*, Willie Boy?" Uncle Al said.

"Huh?" Will said.

"Your friend—he asked if you were better. Better than what—than the last time he saw you?"

"I guess," Will said.

"You know, Will."

Will snuck a glance at the side of Uncle Al's face. It was hardened with the cold air and with determination.

"I was in a bad mood last time he saw me," Will said.

"How bad?"

Could you get off my back? Will wanted to say. He tried to move out of Uncle Al's arm, but he was strong, and Will couldn't budge.

"Okay," Will said stiffly. "Bad enough to punch a fella, but don't tell Mom, okay? She's got enough to worry about."

"I see," Uncle Al said. "You know, if it were me we were talking about at 12 years old, I'd say, 'That's it? You only punched one guy?' But it's you—and I know how Rudolpho raised you. He's not a fighter, and neither are you. So I'm thinking, this fight you got into is serious business."

"A teacher broke it up. It's not gonna happen again."

"How do you know?"

"Because I say it's not," Will said. He couldn't keep the irritation out of his voice.

"If you don't mind my sayin' so, Willie Boy, that isn't going to be enough. Next time some kid gets your goat, you're gonna slug him again—that is, if you're still carrying around this same anger."

Will started to say, "What anger?" but he already knew it was pointless. More than anybody—more than Bud or Mom or Mr. T. or Mrs. Rodriguez—Uncle Al seemed to be able to read his mind. There was also the matter of the band-of-steel arm that was holding him close.

"Yeah, I'm mad," Will said.

"About what I had to tell you about your father."

"Yeah—and that everybody got my hopes all up that God was gonna do this miracle and bring him home. But that's okay, I've just figured out I can't depend on that anymore."

Uncle Al didn't say anything for another block. He just puffed out his breath in frosty clouds as they walked on through the snow, while ahead of them Mom and Fawn's chattering voices filled the silence. When he finally did talk, his words were careful.

"I know your father pretty well. I even remember times when we were kids and he felt a lot like you do—like everything was going wrong and even God couldn't be counted on. I got a feeling he's going through that same thing right now. But I know one thing for a fact because I heard it from one of the rescued prisoners—"

Will stopped dead, snow plowing up around his feet. "Did he know my dad?"

Uncle Al put his hand up. "He did. It's been several months since this fella was at the prison camp, but last time he saw him, your dad was still alive." Uncle Al gave a laugh, and Will was sure he heard tears in it. "In fact, the last time he saw Rudolpho, he was rallyin' the boys, hatching some plan about a pilgrimage."

"A pilgrimage?" Will said. "What's he talking about?"

"There's some chapel, some *santuario*—I don't know much

about Spanish stuff—anyway, there's some special place up in a village called Chimayo. All the men who make it back from the prison are gonna make a pilgrimage—you know, walk 'til they get there—up to this place to thank God they survived."

The tears were so close, Will only knew one way to stop them. "Why didn't you tell us this when you first got here?" he said.

"I told your mother on the way to the restaurant," Uncle Al said. "I wanted to wait until you were ready to hear it."

"I'm always ready to hear about my dad!"

"But you're not always ready to *listen*, Willie Boy. But listen now. Listen like your dad does. If he can count on God, so can you."

"Look—Will—look at this!"

Ahead of them, Fawn was dancing in her boots and pointing to the spectacle in front of them. The hill was dotted with glowing farolitos—a constellation of stars in the snow.

"Isn't that exquisite?" Mom said.

"I'll say." Uncle Al looked down at Will. "Makes me think of hope."

It was about the size of a birthday candle flame, the flicker Will felt inside. It wasn't enough to convince him that God was there to be counted on. But it was enough to get his hackles up again—at the war.

Dad should be here lookin' at this, gettin' ready to paint it. This isn't fair.

He didn't get much further than that until they got home. Uncle Al was stoking the fire and Mom was putting water on for hot tea, and Fawn turned on the radio.

"Hey, Will!" she said. "Listen—it's the Stars Over America Cavalcade people!"

"That's Dorothy Lamour, all right," Uncle Al said. "I'd know that voice anywhere. Now there's a doll if I ever saw one."

"We did see her!" Fawn said.

As she launched into an account of their Cavalcade adventure for Uncle Al, Will listened to Dorothy Lamour's voice. The last time he'd heard it was also one of the last times he'd really felt happy and hopeful.

"Even as I speak," she was saying, "there are two men on the roof of the Metropolitan Opera House. They're camped out there, and they're not coming down until the company raises $500 for bonds! We'll bring our boys home yet!"

You really think so? Will wanted to say to her. *You really think we can make a difference?*

She carried the audience off into a chorus of "Over There," and Will half-listened. The other half of him could hear Uncle Al, back at the farolitos: *Your dad is hatching some plan—*

For the first time in a lot of days, hope got bigger than a birthday candle flame. Maybe, Will thought, maybe he could hatch a plan of his own.

✛ ⚜ ✛

Chapter Nine

*W*ill didn't have much time over the next week to form a clear plan. He kept telling himself over and over: *If my dad can hope, then so can I. If my dad can have a plan, then so can I. I can raise money for lots of bonds to help bring him home. can I.*

But there was too much going on for him to decide on the details of his plan.

Uncle Al left a few days after Christmas to return to Washington. He promised to let them know the minute he heard anything more about Dad.

"Remember what I told you, Willie Boy," he whispered just before he climbed into Bud's ancient Chevy to go to the train station.

As Will watched him go, he was glad they were friends again. But it seemed like his friends were all getting farther and farther away.

Two days before school started again, the Lins moved to Albuquerque. Mom threw a going-away party with all the Japanese food she could concoct from the Mexican-American ingredients available in Santa Fe. It was supposed to give everybody a chance to say good-bye to them, but neither Will nor Kenichi could bring themselves to do it. While Fawn and Emiko were crying and giving each other letters and the stubs of tickets from movies they'd seen together and crying some more, Will and Kenichi had a snowball fight. When Kenichi and his family drove off the next day with everything they owned bursting from the trunk of their car, Will threw one final snowball at the back window and went up to his room for the rest of the day.

Fawn, of course, couldn't leave him alone for long. She came in around ten o'clock and commenced moaning. About the fourteenth time she said, "Life is gonna be so boring without Emi. I love her! I miss her already!" Will pulled out his part of the candy stash Uncle Al had brought and told her to eat up. She was grinning and planning Emiko's first visit before she had the second candy bar down.

I wish it was that easy for me *to feel better*, Will thought. He went back to trying to come up with a plan. It was the only thing that seemed hopeful.

The trouble was, no creative ideas were coming to him. He thought about climbing on top of the house and refusing to come down until—until what? The people who lived here raised $500? Mom would sooner climb up there and shoo him off with a broom.

It occurred to him that even though he wanted to do this on his own, Neddie had a great imagination. He might have some fresh ideas.

But the first day back at school, it was apparent that Neddie wasn't so sure he wanted to be friends with Will anymore. Will and Miguel were sitting at lunch when Neddie passed them with his tray and sat down at the next table—with a bunch of girls.

"Hey, Ned," Will said. "What's the idea?"

"Nothin'," Neddie said. He adjusted his glasses with a nervous finger and went back to his tray.

"What's goin' on?" Will said. "Come sit here."

"Maybe I don't wanna sit there," Neddie said.

"What?" Will said.

"Maybe I don't want you threatening you're gonna drop a wrecking ball on my head again. Maybe next time you'll say you're gonna throw me out the second story window. Or maybe you'll even do it—and maybe I'll break both legs and both arms and be in a body cast and maybe—"

And maybe you've got more imagination than I really need, Will thought.

"Look, I'm sorry," Will said. "I didn't mean to hurt your feelings or something."

"Well, you did, Will Hutchinson," said one of the girls. "So why don't you leave him alone? He's our friend now."

Will gave Neddie a you've-gotta-be-kidding look. Neddie just blinked behind his glasses.

"Never mind," Will said. No self-respecting seventh-grade boy surrounded himself with girls and let them protect him, at least not one in his right mind. Will needed somebody in his right mind.

Will was about to get on the bus for the ride home that afternoon when he heard a familiar horn blowing insistently. It was Bud in the old Chevy, waving him over.

Will's first impulse was to run over to him and hop in. He even started to. But then he remembered his last real conversation with Bud, on the phone, about the pageant.

I already got dumped by one friend today, he thought as he slowed his steps.

But Bud was smiling as he leaned across the tattered seat and creaked open the door on the passenger side for Will.

"Hey, pal," he said. "Long time, no see. How about I treat you to a soda?"

They hadn't been to the Plaza Café together for a long time, and it had once been one of Will's favorite things to do after school. But the hackles were warning him: *He's gonna wanna talk about God. I don't wanna talk about God.*

The thing was, although Uncle Al had convinced him that his father hadn't given up on God, there was no evidence that going back to talking to Him and asking Him for things really made any difference. What made a difference was *doing* something to change things. Doing something yourself. Even Dorothy Lamour had said so.

So Will shook his head and said, "That's okay. I have a lotta homework. I gotta go straight home."

"Hop in, then. I'll give you a lift," Bud said.

There was no way to get out of it without being rude, and both Mr. T. and Mom had made it clear that wasn't one of his choices. With a sigh, Will climbed in.

"So—I hear your Uncle Al brought some encouraging news about your father," Bud said.

"Yeah," Will said.

Bud looked at him curiously. "I thought you'd be more excited."

"It's better not to get your hopes up," Will said. Then he wanted to bite his tongue off. He'd just given Bud the perfect opportunity to start talking about you-know-Who.

But to his surprise, Bud just gave him one more curious look and said, "So what's all this homework they're loading you down with in seventh grade?"

There was no God-talk at all on the ride home, but just to be on the safe side, Will turned down Bud's next couple of invitations during the week to join him for a soda or a movie. He also avoided being alone with Mom, and he definitely watched his step at school so he wouldn't get sent to Mr. T.'s office. He was on his particularly best behavior in Mrs. Rodriguez's class, which didn't turn out to be so hard after the day she made the big assignment.

"Class," she said, "I've been thinking about a conversation we had before Christmas. I believe it was the first day Luis and Pablo and Rafael joined us, if you'll recall."

Who could forget? Will thought. He was still waiting for the Three Amigos to jump him from some dark alley. He was avoiding those, too.

"You'll remember," Mrs. Rodriguez went on, "that we were discussing the treatment of the Indians by the Spanish in the early years of Santa Fe—in particular their attempts to convert the Indians to Christianity." She looked straight at Luis. "I recall that some of you were less than pleased with my version of the tale."

Less than pleased? Will thought. *Luis wanted to start a brawl over it!*

He suddenly felt lonely. If Kenichi were here, Will would be whispering that to him right now, or at least rolling his eyes at him. He tried to catch Neddie's gaze, but he wouldn't look back.

"I've been doing a great deal of thinking about that day," Mrs. Rodriguez said. "And I have decided that you folks need to do some research of your own, just so you will know that I am not making up a story, that I am telling you the truth. Yes, Miguel?"

"We did not question you, Mrs. Rodriguez," Miguel said. "You are the teacher."

Will winced. *Shut up, Miguel. You're askin' for trouble.*

As it was, Luis was already starting to hiss through his teeth.

"I appreciate that, Miguel," Mrs. Rodriguez said, though her eyes were on Luis. "But I think students learn much better when they have to find information out for themselves. So—" She picked up a piece of paper from her desk. "I have assigned each of you a partner, and each set of partners will choose a topic to research and report back on it to the class."

Oh, no, Will thought. *Just my luck, she'll make me work with Pablo—or Luis himself.*

He caught himself starting to pray. This was the kind of situation he used to immediately go to God about. But not now— no God-talk.

"Luis, I want you, Pablo, and Rafael to work together," Mrs. Rodriguez said.

They nodded as if she'd made that decision because she knew what was good for her. Will thought she was nuts. They were never going to get anything done. But at least it was a relief— unless she put Will with one of Neddie's girls.

"Will," she said, "you will work with Miguel."

Will turned around. Miguel's slow smile had appeared with record speed.

"I was hoping for this," Miguel whispered. Will just nodded and kept a wary eye on Mrs. Rodriguez. She'd been good to him on this, but he wasn't going to push his luck. In fact, when she pointed to the list of topic choices on the board, Will was the first to raise his hand.

"Is anything I pick okay with you?" he whispered to Miguel.

Miguel nodded eagerly.

"What'll it be, Will?" Mrs. Rodriguez said.

"Me and Miguel will do the Indians' religion as it was before the Spanish came."

"Good choice. Anyone else?"

"I can get us some good information on this," Will whispered to Miguel as hands went up around them to choose topics.

"But I will work, too," Miguel said. "You will not do it all. We are partners."

"Luis?" Mrs. Rodriguez said. "Has your group selected a topic?"

Luis looked at Rafael, who said, "We don't like none of them topics."

"Interesting. I thought I asked Luis the question."

She gave Luis a hard look, and he managed to sit up a little straighter in his desk.

"Like he told you—" Luis said. "We don't like none of them topics."

"So, you would rather just sit back and gripe."

Rafael gave Pablo a poke and said, "Yeah. That's what we rather do."

"That isn't one of your choices, gentlemen," Mrs. Rodriguez said. "One thing you will learn in my class is that it never helps to merely whine and complain about things. You have to first know what you're talking about and then act on it. If you don't like what I'm teaching about your ancestors—our ancestors— then prove me wrong." She tapped the chalkboard. "You will research the Santuario de Chimayo. A hike up there wouldn't do you any harm. It might use up some of that dangerous energy you three have."

"Rats," Miguel whispered behind Will.

"Why?" Will whispered back.

"I used to live in Chimayo. I know all about the santuario, the chapel, everything. That would have been an easy one, no?"

Will nodded, but suddenly he wasn't really listening to Miguel anymore, or to Mrs. Rodriguez handing out assignments while the Three Amigos muttered under their breaths. He was concentrating on the neon signs going on in his head: *Santuario de Chimayo! That must have been what Uncle Al was talking about—the place where Dad and the other prisoners are going to make their pilgrimage when they get back!*

That's it! Will thought. *I'll hike up there—it can't be too far if Mrs. Rodriguez is telling Luis and them to walk up there. And I'll set up camp and I'll refuse to come home until the town of*

Santa Fe raises the $500 that Fawn promised. I can help bring Dad home and I can show the Three Amigos at the same time!

He was ripping a piece of paper out of his notebook, ready to start planning, when another thought sneaked in, like a tiny voice that had waited for all the others to have their say. *And when you get there, you can thank God for your Dad, that he's still alive. That's what* he *plans to do.*

Will tried to quiet that voice, but it nagged at him. All the rest of the day in school. As he rode the bus home. Past the Red Cross blood drive he couldn't contribute to because he was too young. Past the newspaper stands with their headlines about Iwo Jima and the Battle of the Bulge which he couldn't help with because he was too far away. Past the San Miguel Mission where he couldn't pray because God didn't listen anyway. It was especially then when the voice nagged: *But this plan is* about *God. That's the only reason to do it.*

Will was about to say "shut up," right out loud—and probably get everyone who was left on the bus staring at him—when he spotted a familiar black, silky head on a person on the street. It was Miguel, running as if something—or someone—were after him. Will caught a glimpse of his frightened brown eyes just as he leapt over the mission wall and disappeared.

Will looked out both windows, but he didn't see any sign of Luis or Pablo or Rafael. When the bus stopped at the next corner to let some kids out, Will got off, too, and he ran back to San Miguel Mission, glancing over his shoulders the whole way, but there wasn't a trace of them. If the Three Amigos *had* been after Miguel, he'd successfully given them the slip. Will was impressed.

He jumped over the wall just as Miguel had and looked around. If he was outside, he was well hidden. He had probably gone into the church. Will had his hand on the door handle when he heard a soft voice call out, "Will?"

He turned around to see Miguel standing at the corner of the church.

"Where were you?" Will said. "I didn't even see you back there!"

"Come," Miguel said. "I will show you." He led Will around the corner of the church and pointed to a short set of steps Will had never noticed before. The steps went down to the sidewalk that ran along the side of the church, but the way the slanted stone supports jutted out, a concealed pocket was formed.

"This is my best hiding place," Miguel said. "Come. Join me."

"Swell!" Will said. He sank down onto the steps and was immediately hidden from the Barrio, if not from all of Santa Fe.

"Here we can talk," Miguel said. "Without interruption. You know."

"Yeah, I know. Those fellas are snakes."

Miguel nodded.

"So why aren't you working at LaFonda today?" Will said.

"Since the Christmas crowd has left town, they only have work for me on the weekend," Miguel said. "I do not mind so much, except I have to spend more time protecting myself from—them."

"Why are Luis and those guys out to get you anyway?" Will said. "You just got here, for Pete's sake!"

Miguel looked down at his short body and let his slow smile spread over his face. "Look at me, Weel," he said, pronouncing Will's name in his Spanish accent. "I am—how do I say it— puny."

"No, you're not! Now, Neddie—*he's* puny."

"Still, I am a good target. I wish there was some way I could show them that I am not a coward."

"But you're brave," Will said, "just like your father."

He studied Miguel's face. It definitely wasn't "puny." Right now he looked strong and determined. And he was clever enough to find good hiding places.

And he loved his father, who was away in the war.

If anyone should know how he feels, it's you, Mr. T. had told him.

"You know somethin', Miguel?" Will said. "I think I know just the way. You wanna be partners with me in a plan I'm thinkin' up?"

Miguel didn't even wait to hear what it was. He was nodding his head before Will even got the words Santuario de Chimayo out of his mouth. His eyes were flooded with what Will was pretty sure was hope.

"I can be a great help to you, too," Miguel said, after Will had explained his plan. "I know the place, remember?"

"But that's not the only reason I'm askin' you," Will said.

"I know," Miguel said.

And Will was sure he did.

They began to outline what had to be done right then—find the shortest way to make the 31-mile hike, especially with its last 11 miles being over open, mountainous terrain; decide what food and other supplies to take along; figure out where to hide all the stuff until then; and pick a date.

Miguel was promising to describe the santuario in detail and even draw pictures so they could determine exactly the spot to set up their site, when they heard voices beyond the wall. They got quiet. It was unmistakably Pablo and Rafael, blaming each other for losing Miguel.

Miguel and Will hunkered down and waited for them to pass, grinning at each other in their secret hideaway.

Inside Will, a candle flame grew brighter.

✝ ⸙ ✝

Chapter Ten

*F*rom there, the secret plan began to unfold. Every day after school, Will and Miguel spread out their maps and their lists on Will's bedroom floor, along with their books about ancient Indian religions in Santa Fe. Working on the school project made a great cover.

The route was mapped out easily. Miguel said there was a cutoff at Cuymangue that would take five miles off the trip, but it was a dusty wagon road winding up and down hills and around mesas. It would take longer to stay on the main road, he said, but it was safer. Will argued a little, but Miguel stood his ground. Will was learning that he wasn't as puny as some people thought.

It was easier deciding exactly where they would set up camp and refuse to move until they raised $500. Miguel described the draped altar in the santuario and the high *reredos* behind it decorated with painted symbols. Then he told about the cross that had supposedly been found in a pine tree and was an exact replica of another cross down in Mexico. Legend had it that the people of Chimayo returned the cross to its place in Mexico three different times, and all three times it showed up at Chimayo again. That was all very interesting, but Will wasn't struck with an idea for a spot. It didn't come to him until Miguel talked about Santo Niño Perdido.

"There is a *bulto* behind some curtains," he said.

"What's a *bulto*?" Will said.

"A statue."

"You people sure have a lot of different words for statue," Will said. "*Santos—bultos—*"

"This one is special," Miguel said. "It is a statue of the lost Holy Child."

"You mean, like Jesus?" Will said.

Miguel nodded. "There is a legend about the statue. The people say that every night, the Santo Niño goes out on errands of mercy to the poor, so new shoes must be bought for it every six months."

"You gotta be kiddin'!" Will said. "They really believe that?"

Miguel smiled. "I do not know. But they do not want to take any chances!"

Will nodded vacantly. His mind was busy spinning out the perfect scene.

"So, Miguel," he said. "What if we set up right in front of this bulto thing? We're kind of like lost kids ourselves, you know, with our dads bein' gone and all. And we're on a—what did you call it?"

"Errand of mercy?" Miguel said.

"Yeah—only let's call ours a mission of mercy. Errand sounds too much like my mom's sending me to Roybal's to get a loaf of bread or something."

"Mission of mercy," Miguel said. "I like it."

"Me, too," Will said.

Yeah, everything was unfolding pretty perfectly.

The only problem was Fawn.

With Emiko gone, she was at loose ends, and the minute she came home from St. Catherine's school in the afternoons, she made a beeline for Will's room. He really couldn't blame her for that. Before Ken and Emi had come, he and Fawn had spent every available minute together.

He'd even thought about including Fawn in the plan. She was good at keeping secrets, and her ideas were pretty good, even if she did resort to jumping somebody if things didn't turn out quite her way. Mom often pointed out that they were still working on that.

But the day he got close to inviting her, he remembered why he couldn't.

He and Miguel were in his room, deciding where they were going to hide their supplies until the day they set out for Chimayo, when they heard Fawn hollering all the way from the kitchen downstairs: "Will? You home?"

"Quick!" Will whispered. "Shove the stuff under the bed!"

They were just opening the library book on Native American wisdom when Will's door flew open and Fawn burst in, pigtails flying. Her eyes were alive with whatever news she obviously had to tell.

"Guess what?" she said, instead of hello.

"You kicked some girl's tail on the playground."

"No!"

"Some girl kicked *your* tail on the playground."

"No-o, Will!"

Will winked at Miguel. "You kicked each *other's* tails."

Fawn hurled herself at Will's back and clamped both hands over his mouth from behind. "NO! Listen!"

Will raised his eyebrows at Miguel, who grinned earlobe to earlobe.

"You do not have a choice, my friend," Miguel said.

"Listen," Fawn said. "I'm going to the pueblo—this Saturday!"

Will wriggled out from under her hands on his mouth and twisted his head around to look at her. "I thought you hated going to the pueblo."

"I used to, silly. Not anymore."

"Since when?"

"Since I got the letter from my father. He wants me to go visit and learn about my culture. And I have to because he said so—and he's a hero, you know."

That last part was for Miguel, who made the appropriate impressed sound.

Will gave Fawn a poke. "It's about time you figured that out. Margretta's been tryin' to tell you that all along."

"I know," Fawn said.

She slid off Will's back and planted herself between Miguel and him. Will tried not to glance under the bed to see if she could see stuff. She was sure to pick up on that right away and go diving under there.

"But the *big* reason I didn't want to go out there anymore is because you can't," Fawn said. Her face clouded over. "You don't hate me, do you, because I'm gonna go and you can't? Are you mad that I'm going without you when I said I never would? I know how much you love Quebi—"

"No, I don't hate you," Will said. "And I'm not mad. You gotta do what your dad tells you. If my dad had written me a letter and told me somethin', I'd do it—"

He let his voice trail off. That thought hurt too much to go into it any further.

"Yeah," Fawn said. "I can't get in any trouble—none at all. I know Mama Hutchie wouldn't send me away if I did—she's told me that a buncha times. But I don't wanna disappoint my dad. We're gonna be a real family when he comes back."

Will felt something catch in his throat. *Aren't* we *your family, too?* he wanted to say. *We are! I'll prove it to you. I'll take you on this secret pilgrimage for my dad—*

But the way her eyes were shining, the way she was hugging her knees up to her chest—there was only one real family for Fawn. If she got in trouble, it might ruin everything.

And there was no getting around it—there could be some trouble over the mission. Before Mom would find the note saying where he'd gone, she'd be upset for a short time. She might even be mad until she got up there and saw what he was doing. And knowing Fawn, she wouldn't follow Will's instructions anyway—she was bound to get into some kind of twist.

No, it wasn't worth it. He knew how he'd feel if it was him—trying to be perfect for his dad.

I do know how it feels! he thought suddenly. *'Cause that's what I'm doin'!*

Will shook himself back to the present, where Fawn was filling Miguel in on all the things she was trying to practice for her father.

"A Navajo never steps over another person," she was saying, "so I'm trying not to do that. And Navajos never kill snakes or eat a piece of food with a point of a knife stuck in it. Those are pretty easy. I also have to take care to avoid having beasts cross my path or being around trees that've been damaged by lightning. And I'm especially not supposed to have part of anything that has already died, you know, like a deer that's got hit by a car—"

"I don't think your dad's gonna care about any of that stuff anymore, Fawn," Will said. "He's a Christian now, remember?"

"But those are good things to put in our report, Weel," Miguel said. It was his turn to wink at Will.

"Oh, yeah," Will said. "Tell us some more stuff."

"Can't," Fawn said. "I gotta go read *Laughing Boy.*"

Will stared. "You're gonna read a book—without anybody making you?"

"Yes," Fawn said primly, tossing her pigtails over her shoulders. "Mama Hutchie says it's about the Indians trying to combine their old way of life with the modern world."

It sounded like a speech Fawn had memorized, but Will didn't point that out. She was liable to jump him again.

" 'Course, I could come in here and read," Fawn said.

"Nah, you don't wanna do that," Will said quickly. "You won't be able to concentrate."

"Yeah, I kinda have that problem. It's hard with books. But my dad says I have to get my education, so I'm gonna."

"You are so lucky to have a proud papa," Miguel said.

"You should know!" Fawn said. "I bet your old man's proud of you—the way you play the guitar and talk so proper and everything."

"My 'old man'?" Miguel said.

"That's what my Uncle Al calls a dad," Will said. "Fawn's right. I bet he is proud of you."

Miguel didn't answer. He just looked down at his hands.

"What?" Fawn said. "Is he mean? Doesn't he tell you you're good at playin'? Somebody oughta give him a piece of their mind—"

"Fawn, shut up, would ya?" Will said. "His dad's in the war, just like ours."

"He can still be proud," Fawn said.

"Didn't you say you had to go read?"

"Oh, yeah. I wonder if Mama Hutchie made any cookies?"

When she left, Will locked the door behind her, but he shook his head at Miguel.

"She can be a pest. I don't know how long we're gonna be able to keep this from her, but she can't come. She'd be sure to get in trouble."

"Tomorrow, we can meet at my house," Miguel said. "We will have supper, no?"

"Will!" Fawn hollered from below. "Did you hide the cookies?"

Will nodded at Miguel. "That's a good idea," he said.

So the next morning, Will told Mom, but not Fawn, that he was going to Miguel's and that he'd been invited for supper, and after school he and Miguel walked to the Barrio. The snow had long since melted, and it was warm enough for them to sling their jackets over their shoulders. Will felt adventurous and free, even if he did have to keep an eye out for the Three Amigos. They were keeping suspiciously to themselves these days, and that made him nervous.

Miguel, on the other hand, was too excited about Will coming to his house to seem worried about Luis and his pals. His silky hair bounced as he hurried Will along the brick sidewalk down DeVargas Street.

All the buildings were cream, brown, or reddish-brown adobe with rounded corners and lodgepole-pine vigas sticking out from the inside where they supported the ceilings. There were ceramic tiles everywhere in bright reds and blues and yellows, so that to Will they almost looked like fairy-tale houses. It wasn't the richest part of town; that was obvious from the weathered wooden gates in the adobe walls. But Will liked it. There was so much adobe, drawing in the sun and holding its light, that it felt warm and friendly to him—and it was even more so inside the house Miguel led him into.

There wasn't much furniture within the creamy adobe walls of the front room, which looked as if they'd been rubbed smooth with sheepskin. There were just some low stools, a wooden chest honeycombed with little drawers and compartments and studded with heavy iron hinges and handles, and a long, narrow table with tall, straight, leather-seated armchairs around it.

But the lack of furniture didn't make Will think Miguel was poor. Not only was there a plush carpet on the tiled floor and a mirror framed in gold leaf on one wall, but everything there looked as if it were cared for like it was treasure. Even the vigas that beamed the ceiling, and which were nothing more than the trunks of trees stripped of their bark, looked as if they'd been hand-polished.

While Miguel was putting his books in his bedroom, Will wandered over to a curve-topped inset that had been cut into the thick wall. He'd had one of those in his room in the apartment where he and Mom had lived before they moved into the house on Canyon Road. He had used it for a bookshelf, but this one appeared to be the display case for a small carved statue about eight inches tall. It was almost like a doll—a man-doll dressed in a robe and holding a set of keys.

"You have met Saint Peter," Miguel said as he crossed the carpet behind Will. "He has the keys to the Church, because Jesus put him in charge, no?"

"Is this one of those santos things you were tellin' me about that night at San Miguel?" Will said.

Miguel nodded, looking proud. "My uncle José makes them."

Will studied the statue's dark hair and eyebrows. "If this is Saint Peter, how come he looks so Spanish?"

"It is the tradition. That is my hair you see."

"Yikes!" Will said. "That *is* real hair! And this is actual cloth, too!"

"Uncle José arranges it when it is wet and then paints it when it is dry and stiff. And, you see, the arms move, too."

Miguel pulled Saint Peter's arm up and down gently, as if he didn't want to hurt it. Will chewed at his lip for a second. Then he said, "You know this is just a statue, don't you? I mean, it's not real."

Miguel looked surprised. "I know."

"Okay, well, you're touching it like it's really Saint Peter or somethin'. You did tell me you guys prayed to these things."

"We do not pray TO the statue," Miguel said. "It reminds us of the saint who is so close to God. It helps us to pray."

"Oh," Will said. His hackles were stirring. He really didn't want to get into a discussion of the uselessness of praying. Not here in Miguel's house.

"You may think I am silly, Weel," Miguel said, still fingering the statue. "But I think the faith of my uncle breathes life into the santos."

"This sounds like a deep discussion for a Wednesday afternoon."

Will turned around to see a tall lady enter from one of the rounded doorways, looking every bit as stately as a statue herself. Miguel's face lit up when he saw her.

"Mama!" he said. "I have brought home my friend!"

As she flowed across the room with her graceful hand extended to Will, he wondered if he'd heard right, that this was Miguel's mother. She didn't look like a farmer, that was for sure, and she definitely wasn't like the old Spanish women in town who walked around with their black rebozos over their heads and shoulders.

She had lighter skin than most of the Spanish people he knew who worked the fields, and her hair, which was tightly wavy, was parted neatly in the middle and pulled back into a bun at the nape of her neck, almost like a movie star. Her upper lip even made the top of a heart.

"This is Weel Hutchinson," Miguel said. "My friend."

The pride in his voice made Will feel a little shy, as if he were sure he couldn't live up to Miguel's opinion of him. But his mother seemed to buy into it right away as she grasped Will's hand between her two warm, slender ones and said, "It is a pleasure to meet you, Will."

There was no mistaking where Miguel got his proper speech. Every word was as precise as a note on a flute, and she had less of an accent than Miguel did.

"Hi," Will said. "Um, what should I call you?"

"Señora Otero will be fine," she said. Then she drew her thick, dark eyebrows together the same say Miguel did when he was concentrating and added, "I hope Miguel has been a good host. Has he offered you something to eat?"

"Not yet, but he's a swell host," Will said. He suddenly wished he'd paid more attention in English class. Between her and Miguel, he felt like an uneducated hobo talking.

"Well, if you can wait just a little longer, I will prepare supper for us," Señora Otero said. "I want to finish my poem. Miguel, since Will is so interested in the santos, why do you not take him out to see your uncle? He is at work on some new ones."

Señora Otero swept back across the room and disappeared through the rounded arch.

"Your mom reads poetry?" Will said. "I don't think my mom ever does that."

"No," Miguel said. "She writes it."

"Oh," Will said. "Jeepers."

Miguel led the way out a windowed door to a large patio which even in the middle of winter was dotted with green plants. Will figured anything would grow with the beautiful Señora Otero coaxing it. The thought made his ears turn red.

There were several large wooden doors on the other side of the patio, and Miguel opened one of them. Will was immediately caught up in the smells of freshly cut wood and charcoal and clay.

In the center of the room they stepped into was a high, thick table, and behind it sat a man Will thought must be a hundred years old. His long face was covered in crusty gray-white whiskers that included a bushy moustache. Longish hair, cut much the way Miguel's was, fell over his weathered, wrinkled forehead, nearly touching his thick eyebrows which were still very black except for the few gray hairs that grew like strays between them over his very-large nose.

He looked so old and wizened, Will was almost afraid for him to look up. People that old, in his experience, were usually cranky. But the eyes that looked up at him gleamed just like Miguel's. Will knew then he could only be about 50. It was just the way his flesh drew up in wrinkles over his large bones that made him look old and gaunt. No, the eyes that smiled at Will were young.

"This is my uncle José, the *santero*," Miguel said, with that same proud tone in his voice that he used for everything he obviously loved. "*Tio,* this is my friend, Weel."

Uncle José stood up—and up and up. Will was amazed at how tall he was and how large was the hand that came out to grasp his. How, he wondered, could hands that big do such small work?

"Tio doesn't speak much English," Miguel said in a low voice. "But he understands everything we say."

"I don't," Will said. "What's a tio?"

"That's Spanish for uncle," Miguel said.

Uncle José's eyes smiled and he sat back down on his stool.

"Weel wants to know about the santos, Tio."

Uncle José nodded and went back to his work. Miguel picked up a rounded wooden doll that had no features or clothes yet, or even any arms or legs.

"This is a bulto," Miguel said. "He makes the body from this, and then the arms and legs are attached with these strips of cloth, pasted on like hinges. This one over here he has covered with gypsum wash—" Miguel pointed to a white, naked-looking doll. "And the one he is working on right now, he is painting the eyes and the mouth and the flesh."

"Who's that one gonna be?" Will said.

Uncle José said something in Spanish.

"That's Michael. I don't know them until they have their tools. See, I know all of these."

He went over to a shelf that contained more santos than Will could count at the moment. Each one was dressed differently and held something different in its hand. Miguel did know them all. Raphael had a fish, Veronica a veil, and John had a long staff and a lamb.

"Does he make all these little toy things that they're holding, too?" Will said.

"Their tools? Yes. Every tiny one."

"How did he learn how to do this stuff?"

"My great-grandfather, Uncle José's father, taught him, and his father before him taught him. And *he* learned from one of the monks, because all the santos that were brought here from the old country were destroyed in the Pueblo Revolt, and the monks did not want the Spanish people to lose their culture."

"I guess there was a lot of that going around."

Will leaned in to look at the faces on the small figures again. There was something about their eyes that did seem real—only, of course, they weren't. What *was* it?

"Their faces are so thin," he said out loud. "That's why their eyes look big. It's like they're really lookin' at you."

Uncle José said something else in Spanish, a long something this time, and his eyes glowed as he talked. They looked a lot like the ones on the statues.

"What did he say?" Will whispered when Uncle José went back to his work.

"He said the faces are thin because the saints experienced poverty and hardship in their lives, but they still found peace with God. We are to do the same."

"Oh," Will said.

He was glad that just then, Señora Otero put her head in the door and said, "Supper is ready."

The four of them sat at the long table in front of the big windows that faced out onto the patio—the *placita,* Señora Otero called it. She served them paella, which was a rice dish Will had had before, only this was different. It tasted strong, and it seemed to bite back with every mouthful. Will got used to it quickly, the way the green chilies burned his mouth and his chest in a pleasant, zesty kind of way, and he devoured two helpings along with the *posole,* a brown-crusted bread that had been toasted with butter and garlic and grated cheese. He was almost moaning, he was so full, when Señora Otero brought in the chocolate cake, but he polished off a piece of that, too.

It wasn't just the food that made the supper good. It was the way the tin behind the oil lamps reflected their light, and the way the fire crackled in their kiva in the corner, and the way Miguel and his mother talked and laughed as if the war wasn't even happening. Will himself almost forgot about it until later, when he and Miguel were spread out at the table with their two projects, while Señora Otero went back to her poetry, and Uncle José returned to his work. Will was staring into space, trying to come up with the best way to wrap their tent so that it wouldn't be found under the stairs in San Miguel Chapel, where they'd decided to hide it until their trip, when he noticed a framed photograph on top of the big chest.

It pictured a man in a uniform, and that drew Will's attention right away. When he got up to get a closer look, he realized that the officer in the photo had the same insignia on his uniform that Dad had on his.

"Is this your father?" Will said to Miguel.

At once, Miguel's chair scraped back over the tile floor and he was at Will's side, taking the picture from him.

"Yes, but do not talk about it," he whispered to Will, and put the picture back on top of the chest.

"How come?" Will whispered back, although he wasn't sure why they were talking in hushed voices.

"It makes Mama upset," Miguel said. "Please—no more talk of my father."

Then he set his strong little face and sat back down. Will decided that wasn't the time to ask if Señor Otero could be in the 200th Coast Artillery like Dad.

Boy, I thought I was riled up about the war. These people won't even talk *about it!*

No wonder Miguel wanted to make this trip so badly.

All right then, Will decided. *It's going to be a success. And we aren't just doing it for the money.*

He almost let the thought slip in that they were doing it for God. But he pushed that aside and looked over at the statue of Saint Peter.

It does about as much good to talk to God as it does to one of these statues, he thought.

And he was more determined than ever to go on this mission—he and Miguel—on their own.

✝ ⚜ ✝

Chapter Eleven

*F*or the next week, even on the weekend, Will and Miguel continued to make their plans. Fawn spent almost every afternoon at the pueblo—thanks to Bud and his old but faithful Chevy—and Señora Otero and Uncle José were always busy with their own work, so the two boys were able to work in the privacy of Miguel's tiny bedroom, on the other side of the placita from the main house.

Once in a while, they slipped into the kitchen for bocadillos, which were a lot like sandwiches, or one of Señora Otero's small sweet puddings, and occasionally they stopped in at the shop to see how the santos were coming along. But most of the time, they were making their maps, gathering their supplies using Will's allowance and some of Miguel's guitar-playing money, and making trips to San Miguel. By the 20th of January, the bell tower, the pockets under the pews, and even some of the larger statues were protecting rolls of sleeping bags and blankets and cans of beans and, of course, can openers.

Once, when the two boys were up in the bell tower adding

some more blankets to their packs, they heard one of the monks coming onto the balcony just below them.

"Should we hide?" Will whispered.

Miguel shook his head and, grabbing Will by the arm, pulled him out of the tower and down the steps. On the balcony, the monk began pulling on the bell rope, and Will didn't even have to ask why Miguel had hauled him out of there so fast. He covered his ears until they were outside the front door.

"We do not want to be in the bell tower when the bell rings," Miguel said as they slipped into their hideaway.

"No kiddin'?" Will said. "A person could go deaf!"

"It will give you a headache you will never forget," Miguel said. "Once my cousin tried to—" He stopped and shook his head. "There is not time to speak of that now. We must decide on a day for our mission to begin."

That was the only thing left to do, and they put their heads together.

Meanwhile, things began to go better at school, even without Will's noticing it at first.

Mrs. Rodriguez took Will out into the hall one day while the class was taking a test and commended him for working so well with Miguel. At least now he knew what commended meant, and he could thank her. Besides, it wasn't that hard working with Miguel. He was Will's best friend in school now. Neddie, it seemed, was becoming too much of a ladies' man.

Another day Mr. Tarantino stopped Will in the hall when he was hurrying to class. Although Will apologized immediately for half-running in the hall, Mr. T. shook his head and smiled down at him. He, too, had a commendation for him.

"I can see the old Will is returning," he said. "He's welcome to come to my office for a visit any time. Purely a social call, of course."

"Sure," Will said. But he didn't intend to do it, at least not right away. He was afraid he'd give the secret of the santuario trip away, and that would spoil everything.

The Three Amigos, it turned out, almost did spoil everything. Just when Will was sure their little "talks" with Mr. T. after school were paying off and they had given up the idea of getting back at Will, they proved him wrong.

It was January 22, lunchtime. Will and Miguel were sitting near the window in the cafeteria, watching the snow fall to the north of them.

"If it is snowing when we go," Miguel said, "it will be hard for us to hike, especially the last 11 miles."

"We'll just have to wait for a clear day," Will said. "We want everything perfect for our dads, right?"

Miguel didn't answer. His gaze had shifted to a spot over Will's shoulder, and his eyebrows were knitting together.

"Luis?" Will mouthed to him.

Miguel gave a nod so small it didn't even move his silky hair.

For the first time in weeks, Will could feel his hackles beginning to stir. Why did they have to start something up now, just when everything was going so well?

"Hey," he heard Rafael say behind him. "It's the Anglo and the Sissy. They make a nice couple, eh?"

Will turned around just in time to see him exchange pokes with Pablo. Luis was paying no attention to them. He seemed to have eyes only for Will. The hackles stood up straighter.

"What do you want, Luis?" Will said. "We're havin' a private conversation here."

"About what?" Rafael said.

Luis hushed him with a hiss.

"So?" Will said. "Are you just gonna stand there, or are you gonna tell us what you want? We got things to do."

"You right, An-glow," Luis said, in a voice much louder than the one he usually used. "You got somethin' to do. You gotta raise $500 like you promised in front of the whole town."

There was a stir in the cafeteria, which was apparently just what the Three Amigos wanted, because even Luis looked back at the crowd with a smile.

"I don't see what business that is of yours, Luis," Will said. "We promised the town, not you."

"I don't live in this town?" he said.

"Yeah, he does," said another voice. Will all but rolled his eyes straight back into his head. It was Neddie. Fortunately, two of his girl pals shushed him up. Luis acted as if he hadn't heard.

"I told you, An-glow—someday I was gonna make sure everybody knows what a bragger and a liar you are—just so you will be a disgrace like you try to make me." His gash of a smile cut across his face. "Today is someday."

Thoughts, the right thoughts, were all hammering for attention in Will's head.

He's all talk. Ignore him.

Get up and walk away.

Pray, Will. Pray for the right words.

But all his attention was pulled away by the prickling at the back of his neck. His anger was up, and that was all he could hear. He stood up and faced Luis, nose to nose.

"How do you know I don't already have a plan for raising the money?" he said.

"Because you a liar. Last year, when you cheated me—you a liar then. You a liar now."

"That *is* true," said somebody in the crowd. "Will even told the class he lied. Last year—"

A separate discussion ensued. Luis shut it out with a jerk of his head. "You are lying," he said.

"No, I'm not," Will said through his teeth. He was trying with everything in him not to haul off and punch Luis, but it was getting harder by the second.

"Prove it, then," Luis said.

The crowd began licking its chops. The only person Will saw was Miguel. His eyebrows were one, and his eyes were huge— just like the eyes of the santos. Slowly, almost without moving, he was shaking his head. Will snapped his eyes back to Luis.

"I don't have to prove anything to you, Luis," he said. "I got plans, that's all I gotta say. If you don't believe me—"

"I don't," Luis said.

"So what?" Will said. His voice was still strong, but he could feel himself sagging. If he didn't get those hackles back up, Luis was going to walk all over him.

"I will show you what," Luis said. He put his hands up to his jacket lapels and pulled them back. Immediately, like two body-guards, Pablo and Rafael stepped up and peeled his jacket off of him. Boys shoved chairs and tables out of the way. Girls squealed and dove for the walls, heads still craning to see.

Will stayed still. He didn't have to look at Miguel to know that he was shaking his head, and hard this time. Will wanted to shake his, too. There were still hackles, but there was also the desperate cry in his head—*don't do this or you're going to spoil everything. You'll never get to Santuario de Chimayo.* He couldn't fight. But he couldn't walk away, either.

"You gonna fight me, An-glow?" Luis said. He already had his fists at the ready and his feet in fight-stance.

"No," Will said.

The crowd gave a disappointed groan.

"But I will tell you this," Will went on. "By Monday morning, I will have $500. Maybe even more. I'm not a liar, Luis. And I'll prove it to you."

The crowd was obviously not as happy with that decision as they would have been if Will had gone a couple of rounds with Luis. But it gave them something to talk about as Will nodded to Miguel and they wove their way through the kids and out of the cafeteria. Behind them, Will could hear Rafael yelling, "Don't believe it. He *is* a liar—a rotten, stinkin'—"

The door closed on his voice, but he wasn't the only one who was mad. Miguel's eyes were as close to fiery as Will had ever seen them.

"Why did you do that, my friend?" he said. "There is snow! How are we—"

"I don't know," Will said. "But we're gonna have to find a way. We have to leave tomorrow."

That afternoon, they made a final check of their supplies and equipment at San Miguel Mission, but most of the excitement had gone out of the plan. Miguel barely talked at all as they made sure everything was still safely tucked into place for tomorrow morning's pickup. Finally, Will couldn't stand it any longer.

"You're mad at me, aren't you?" he said.

Miguel studied the seat of the pew they were sitting in. It took him a long time to answer.

"Not mad, Weel," he said finally. "I am disappointed. I thought we were doing this thing to honor our fathers—raise money for the war to be over."

"We still are," Will said.

"No. Now we are doing it to prove ourselves to Luis."

"Don't you want to show him that you aren't a sissy? That's all he talks about, and he and his friends chase you all over. You never have a minute's peace."

"I do not like that, no," Miguel said. His eyebrows were nearly in a knot as he searched Will's face. "But what does it matter what we do? They will never change—I know this."

"How?" Will said.

Miguel pressed his lips together.

"What? Do you know somethin' about them that I don't know?"

"I know if we do this to prove ourselves to them, we take

them with us. I do not want them with us."

"Okay," Will said. His stomach was churning. If Miguel backed out, there would be no trip. He couldn't do it alone, and he knew that. "Okay, forget about them. From this moment on, no more talking about the Three Amigos. It's just you and me and our dads." He forced a grin. "No?"

Whether Miguel knew his heart was pleading, Will couldn't tell. But slowly, Miguel let his smile appear.

"I believe you. We do this for the fathers. We do this for the war. We do this for God."

Will just nodded. Above them, the San José bell began to chime for five o'clock, and he stood up.

"I gotta get home," he said. "You comin'?"

Miguel shook his head. "I will stay here and pray," he said.

"Oh," Will said. He felt a tug inside, a tug to sit back down, to get on his knees even. But instead he said, "We meet at five A.M., right? Exactly 12 hours from now, right here."

"I will be here," Miguel said.

As Will hurried out of the chapel, he wondered if Miguel were going to sit there and pray *until* tomorrow morning.

No more God-talk, he told himself firmly. *None.*

But it turned out that was impossible. He and Mom and Fawn had no sooner finished supper—during which Fawn spilled her milk, dropped half her beans on the floor, and finally had to be excused for giggling uncontrollably—than there was a knock on the back door. Will froze automatically. Somebody unexpected always made him afraid it was a telegram.

But it was Bud, and at this point, that was almost as bad as far as Will was concerned. Will missed him—missed their sodas and movies and talks and even the beat-up old car. But he'd been avoiding Bud, giving him every excuse he could think of. Sooner or later the whole praying topic was going to come up.

This time, however, there was no avoiding him. The minute

Bud said, "Will, how 'bout a soda?" Mom was up getting Will's coat and practically putting it on him. Will smelled a trap, and there was no way out of it.

"Sure," Will said, glaring at Mom. "I could go for a soda, I guess."

"Don't worry about the hour," Mom said. "Stay out as late as you want."

"I gotta get some sleep!" Will said, before he could stop himself.

"Tomorrow's Saturday," Mom said. Then her mouth started to twitch, and she covered it with her hand.

"What?" Will said.

"Nothing," Mom said. "Go have a good time."

"Her and Fawn," he complained to Bud as they walked to the car. "They're both going looney."

Bud chuckled. "Sounds like you need a *double* malt."

They were settled into a red leather booth at the Plaza Café with double chocolate malts in front of them when the dreaded subject came up. And this time, Bud wasn't taking no for answer.

"I'm sure you feel like I practically tied you up and dragged you here," Bud said. "I had to get your mother to scheme with me. Don't be too hard on her."

"Nah," Will said. "I know why you did it. You wanna talk about God and praying and stuff. Can I just say, I don't?"

"You can say it," Bud said. "And you don't have to talk if you don't want to. But I am going to ask you to listen."

There was nothing Elmer Fudd about him now. His pale, pudgy face was serious. It looked like Will really didn't have a choice.

I don't have to buy it, he told himself. *'Cause I already know better.*

"I'm not going to pretend I know what's going on in your mind," Bud said. "But I think I know it has something to do with you not trusting God so much anymore. Am I right?"

"Yeah," Will said. "And you aren't gonna—"

"Just hear me out," Bud said. "I don't blame you for feeling that way. We adults are asking a lot of you kids in this war. The expectations we have of you are, well, they're extraordinary. We all have a sense of purpose because of the war, but I know it's robbing you kids of what you really want. And what you really want, Will, is your father here. Right?"

Will nodded. "And I already asked God to bring him home with the other rescued prisoners, and He didn't. All that proves to me is that God doesn't give you what you want."

He waited for Bud's voice to get stern. After all, even mild-mannered pastors had their limits. But to his surprise, Bud nodded, too.

"In some cases, that's true," Bud said. "God doesn't always give you what you want just because you ask Him for it."

"Then what's the point in even asking?" Will said.

Bud closed his eyes and sat back against the booth, his head touching the mirror behind it. "I've been waiting for weeks for you to ask me that," he said. "Again, you don't have to agree with my answer—just listen."

Will abandoned his malt and folded his arms on the table's black top. "All right," he said. "I'll listen."

"You know that Tina and I are trying to adopt Abe so we can keep him—forever. He's always going to need parents and constant care, no matter how old he gets. We thought everything was going just fine and the adoption would be final in a few months, but we've gotten tangled up in some red tape. Now, Tina and I want that boy more than anything in this world. If he were taken away from us—"

Will sat straight up. "They can't take Abe away!"

"Yes, they can, and they might. And sometimes I get pretty mad about it and sometimes Tina cries because she's sure they're going to come in the middle of the night and drag him off. The point is, though, neither one of us is giving up. We pray constantly."

"But you just said that doesn't automatically mean God's gonna change things."

"Right. Prayer doesn't always change the situation to what we want, but it always changes us, and for the better."

Will tried not to roll his eyes. "I don't get it," he said.

"When you pray, no matter what the outcome, you get closer to God. Then God can help you cope with the situation, even if it doesn't turn out the way you want it to."

"I don't need that," Will said, raising his chin. "I'm doing just fine on my own."

"Are you?" Bud said.

"Yes," Will said.

"Which is why you got into a fight at school—wouldn't participate in the Christmas pageant—"

"I'm over that now!" Will said.

Bud stopped and took a long drink out of his malt glass. When he set it down, he said, "I hope so, Will. But promise me one thing?"

"I don't know," Will said. "Maybe."

"Okay, then just promise me you'll think about this: If you find out you're not doing just fine on your own, stop right then and pray, not just in words, but right from your heart. God's already waiting for you to do that."

"I'm not so sure about that," Will said. "No offense or anything, but God's not that close right now."

"Maybe not," Bud said. "But who moved, you or Him?"

Will shrugged.

"I do know. And I know the minute you even look like you want to talk to Him, He's there. Matter of fact, if you'll look at the last few weeks, there have probably been plenty of times when He was there, working with you, even when you weren't paying attention. So, is it a promise?"

Will looked at him over the top of his malt glass. "Will you drop the subject if I promise to think about it?"

"Absolutely."

"Okay, then I promise to *think* about it. *If* I feel like I'm not doing fine."

"Let's drink to it," Bud said. And they clinked glasses.

Later on, as he was trying to get to sleep, Will thought about that promise.

I'm not gonna have to keep it, he told himself. *Because I really* am *doing fine, and I'm gonna keep doing fine. Tomorrow's gonna be great.*

He turned over with a smile, expecting to doze right off. But his mind came alive with arguments.

It's still snowing up there; you know that, don't you?

You think Miguel's prayers will work, even though you didn't pray?

There have *been a lot of good things happening lately. Maybe Bud's right. Maybe that's God, even though you're not talking to Him.*

"Now I know why everybody's always telling me to stop arguing," he muttered. "I'm driving *myself* crazy!"

He "drove" until nearly one A.M., and he was making up for lost sleep when someone shook him.

"Will! Will—wake up!"

Will opened bleary eyes to see Fawn on her knees on his bed.

"What?" he said. "It's the middle of the night!"

"No—it's four o'clock. Get up!"

Will's mind slipped into gear, and he sat straight up. "Why?"

he said. "Fawn, were you snooping in my stuff?"

"No, silly," she said. "It's San Ildefonso Festival Day at the pueblo and you get to go!"

✢ ✢ ✢

o!" Will said. He rubbed his eyes and said it again. "No!"
Fawn bounced on the bed. For the first time Will realized that she was already dressed, boots and all.

"I knew you were gonna be excited," she said. "I've been about to pop keeping this a secret."

"I can't go," Will said.

"Yes, you can. Every time I've been out to the pueblo I've been begging Quebi, and he finally got me a talk with the governor. I told him how much you've changed and how you really do respect their culture—and that you're even doing a report on it. Finally they said yes!"

"Quebi wants to see me?"

"Of course! You might not get to actually talk to him because there's the dances going on, but you'll at least get to see him. Come on, get dressed. Mama Hutchie's already ridden the motorcycle over to Bud's to get the car. He's lending it to us for the day." She giggled, a sound he hadn't heard from her since Emiko moved away. "Everybody in the whole world knew about this except you!" she said, and then she flew out the door.

Not everybody, Will thought miserably. *Not Miguel.*

He yanked his sweater and dungarees on over his pajamas and headed down the stairs to call him, even if it meant waking up his mother and Uncle José. Will was halfway down the stairs before he remembered that Miguel didn't have a phone.

He stopped on the bottom step and tried to gather his thoughts.

He could try to run to the Barrio and tell Miguel and then run back before Mom got back with Bud's car. The sound of the ancient Chevy already pulling into the driveway squashed that plan.

He could write a note to Miguel and throw it out the car window as they passed San Miguel Chapel and hope Miguel found it.

There were so many problems with *that*, Will didn't even give it a second thought. There was only one thing to do, and that was go on to the pueblo and pray that Miguel would know when he got to San Miguel Chapel that something had happened that couldn't be helped.

Will caught his breath. Had he just told himself to pray?

"Quiet, Bud," he muttered, and went on to the kitchen.

Mom was almost as excited as Fawn. Both of them were donning scarves, gloves, ear muffs, and polar bear style coats and giggling, as if Mom had taken Emiko's place. Will felt a little sad. A month ago, he would have been jumping up and down with them.

The ride to San Ildefonso Pueblo was the longest ever, between the wartime speed limit being only 35 miles per hour and the snow that was still softly falling, and Will's thoughts pulling him back to Santa Fe and Miguel.

Any other time he would have been daydreaming about the big red rock formations that rose on either side of the highway like hills that had lost their tops, but now he was only imagining Miguel sitting all alone in the back of the church.

When on a different day he would have gotten happily lost in thought gazing out at the brooding silence of the big, snowy land, today he was driven nearly to jump out the window by thoughts of how he was going to explain all this to his friend.

They were turning into the long, now-slushy road that led from the highway into San Ildefonso when he had the worst thought yet: There would be no $500 to show Luis on Monday. The whole school was going to think he was a liar.

When Mom parked the car just inside the pueblo entrance, Will slowly climbed out. When once he would have taken off for the plaza with winged feet, now he felt like a sack of lead.

Fawn, on the other hand, had not stopped talking for the entire 22-mile ride, and she was now pointing out everything to Mom.

"See how they just whitewashed all the buildings for the feast day?" she said. "I got to help. That big field there, that's the plaza. That's where the dance is gonna be. Most of the time, if you're not an Indian you don't get to walk on that because it's sacred ground—"

She went on to tell Mom about the kiva, and Will looked sadly around. The pueblo was almost exactly as he remembered it, with the one big cottonwood on the bare plaza, the rounded hills dotted with snow-covered piñons and juniper hovering on the east, and the Black Mesa standing square and solid at the edge of the frozen Rio Grande.

But some things were very different. He'd never seen it powdered with snow before. Although it turned the towering cottonwood into an ice castle, it only made him think of the trek he and Miguel were supposed to be making right now, up to Chimayo.

He had also never been there on a festival day before, and

there was a quiet, almost silent excitement in the air that brought the usually sleepy pueblo to life. There wasn't a person on the plaza as Fawn led them to it, dancing with every step. When they reached the spot she'd picked out for them to sit with their blankets, she said to Will, "You aren't as excited as I thought you'd be."

"I'm just cold," Will said. That was partly true. The sun hadn't even come up yet, and his breath stiffened in the air as he breathed.

Fawn tossed him another blanket. "I just thought you'd be jumping out of your skin, that's all," she said. Her face went saggy.

She looked so disappointed, Will forced himself to smile. "I'm still in shock," he said. "This was a big surprise, remember?"

"I got you good, didn't I?" she said, and the grin spread across her face again.

"Yeah," Will said. "You sure did."

He was glad when Fawn's eyes suddenly lit on something behind him. He turned to see a familiar figure hurrying toward them, wrapped in a bright Indian blanket and wearing white deerskin boots. But she wasn't an Indian. She was Margretta Dietrich.

"Mama Hutchie!" Fawn cried. "Look who's here!"

"For heaven's sake!" Mom said.

"You don't think I'd miss a feast day, do you?" Margretta said. Her mouth went into its line of a smile. "The food is far too good!"

Fawn was tugging at her arm. "What about my mom? Does she know I got a letter from Shush?"

Mom nudged Will. "I don't think he has to worry anymore about Fawn embracing her culture," she said.

"Your mother is wonderful," Margretta said. "Her sight has been almost completely restored, and while she's been there, they've discovered a couple of other health problems, which they're clearing up. She should be ready to come back to Santa Fe by summer—and you aren't going to believe the change in her."

"Shush'll be home long before that!" Fawn said. "Yikes! I gotta get to work on that wedding dress!"

Margretta looked mystified, but there was no more time for questions. Margretta pointed toward the curve of the nearest hill, where Will saw the tiny figure of a man with the beginnings of daylight coming up behind him.

"Ah," Margretta said quietly. "Soon they'll come over that hill—all kinds of animals."

"Real ones?" Will whispered.

"Watch," Margretta said. Then she reached over and squeezed his hand. "It's good to see you again, my smart young friend."

Close behind them, a deep Indian drum began to beat. Four old men took their places on the plaza. Will was at first disappointed that they weren't wearing special costumes, except for the bright headbands that kept their braided hair neatly in place. But his disappointment faded when he saw that one of them was Quebi.

It was all Will could do not to call out to him. As it was, he drank in every line in Quebi's deep-creased brown face.

The four men tilted their heads back and began to chant—not so differently from the monks in San Miguel Mission. Their eyes closed as if they were praying, and their mouths formed perfect O's.

Behind them, women and children gathered and formed two columns as they looked up to the hill as if they were expecting something. Will wanted to look, too, but he had trouble taking his eyes off of Quebi.

"What's Quebi singing?" he whispered to Margretta.

"They're singing for all people," Margretta said. "They're

asking for good things for this pueblo and for all people every-where. The Indians tell me, though, that to them it isn't only the words of the prayer, but how they say them, that's important. They have to come from a singing heart." She glanced up. "Look, Will."

She nodded toward the hill, where the ground had suddenly come alive. Two deer—men dressed as deer—came over the crest with antlered heads and zigzagged down the hill.

Next were buffalo-men, bare to the waist even in the cold and painted with symbols. Their huge headdresses were made of twigs and horns, but it took only a few seconds for Will to believe they were buffalo heads.

The "antelope" who followed were slender children, dressed in what looked like yellow-dyed long underwear.

You'll be wearing those next year, Fawn, Will thought to himself as he stifled a snort.

But the antelope-children were every bit as precise in their movements as the men who came after them with evergreens around their wrists and knees.

"Those are the hunters," Margretta said. "They're thanking the animals for laying down their lives for the sake of all the living, and they're promising to take life only when it's needed for food."

Just then the "animals" began their parade through the two columns of people. As they passed, looking very dignified, Will thought, the Indians began throwing something at them.

"What is *that?*" Will whispered.

"Sacred meal," Margretta said. "They're celebrating their be-lief that the ancient magic has worked once more."

Will was about to ask "what magic?" but the animals and Quebi and the other older men were disappearing into a small house on the south plaza.

"That was swell," Will said.

"But that's not all," Margretta said. "Just wait until they come out of the Deer House."

They spent the next 30 minutes waiting and trying to stay warm. Although daylight now filled the sky, the air was still icy and snow-filled, and they all had to huddle together in their blankets to ward off the cold. But when the door of the small house opened, all thoughts of frozen fingers and toes disappeared.

A figure in a blanket stepped out, and a thrill went through Will because it was Quebi. Behind him came the dancers, their bodies painted with black and white circles and spots, red yarn flowing from their legs as their moccasin-clad feet lifted and then came down to beat the earth.

Soon all the dancers were out on the plaza, their legs moving as if they were one person, their embroidered skirts and their "tails" of fox skin twirling as they danced. They wore large evergreen collars around their necks and red feathers in their hair, which drew Will's eyes right to their faces. Every one of them wore the same expression as they chanted their prayer and moved with the earth they were celebrating.

For a long time they danced, making a square around the plaza. When finally they disappeared into the house again, Will had the urge to clap, but Margretta put her hands on his and smiled.

"Sorry," Will said.

"Not to worry," Margretta said. "So, how did you like it?"

"I did like it," Will said. "Only . . . I don't know what to say."

"That's a first," Mom said, mouth twitching. "But I know what you mean. There are no words to describe what we just saw." She leaned in close, so she could speak into Will's ear. "The Indians are expressing their faith," she said. "It isn't the same as following Christ, but if only we could accept what we can't put into words about Jesus with that same total trust."

Will looked at his mom. Even though she was smiling at him, she looked somehow sad.

Even more excitement followed throughout the day. There was a Comanche Dance, which Margretta said had become a tradition two centuries before when the natives had turned back the Comanche Indians in a raid.

There were also songs and a feast of squash and beans and meat stew with purple onions, as well as more small dances, everything done with fun and laughter among the Pueblo people. Margretta said it was all done to bring the Indians into harmony with nature. Will was about to ask what *that* meant, when Fawn ran up to him and tugged so hard on his arm he thought she'd yank it out of the socket.

"Will!" she said. "Quebi wants to see you!"

"Me?" Will said.

"He knows you're here and he sent me to get you. Come on!"

For once Will didn't argue with her. He followed her eagerly to what he remembered was Quebi's house.

"I'll see ya later," Fawn said at the door. "He wants to see you alone."

For a scared second, Will almost changed his mind. If Quebi wanted to see him alone, it might mean he was disappointed in him. Maybe Fawn had told him Will had been getting into trouble. If that was the case, Will wasn't sure he wanted to hear what Quebi had to say. He didn't want to ruin this day.

But when he glanced inside the two-room house with its smooth dirt floor, Quebi was already watching him.

"Boy," Quebi said. His mouth was curved down at the corners, but his voice was soft and low, just like always.

"Hello, Quebi," Will said. And he smiled and went inside.

Quebi was sitting next to a small fire, and he beckoned for Will to join him. Will sat across from him and waited. There was a long pause.

I remember this, Will thought. *They like to be quiet.*

For the first time in a long time, the silence didn't bother Will. He took a deep breath and settled into his sit. Around him the walls were white and smooth, and the ceiling was upheld by plain pine beams. It felt simple and safe.

"You are cold," Quebi said finally.

"No—the fire feels good," Will said.

The lines on either side of Quebi's long nose deepened. "You are cold here." He put his hand on his chest.

"Oh," Will said.

There was another long pause. This one wasn't so comfortable.

"I guess it's because I'm worried about my father," Will said.

"You speak of this to your God?" Quebi said.

Will couldn't help but stare. He'd forgotten how clearly Quebi seemed to see right into his mind.

"No," Will said. "I don't pray anymore. God doesn't answer."

The pause was shorter. "In Indian life, man must follow prayer to point of knowing. Then he will find answer."

"I don't understand."

Quebi observed the fire as if the answers were there.

"Boy see trail he does not know," he said. "Footprint of stranger. Follow to point of knowing."

"You mean, like my pilgrimage?" he said.

Quebi tilted his head, and Will told him about the plan to hike to the Santuario de Chimayo. It was the first time he'd thought about it since this morning, and once more he felt anxious and disappointed.

"So I couldn't even follow that to the—what did you call it?" Will said. "The point of knowing?"

"At end of journey," Quebi said, "you will thank your God?"

"Not exactly," Will said slowly. "Mostly we're going to raise money for war bonds. Do you know about those?"

"I know white man take work of war from hands of God," Quebi said after a pause.

"But aren't we supposed to help?" Will said. "Besides, God wasn't doing anything. I have to—"

He stopped. Quebi's face had grown drawn and solemn. For the first time, what Will had been thinking about God didn't make so much sense.

"Indian prays to point of knowing."

Then Quebi sat back and his lines smoothed. Will knew the conversation was over. But the discussion in his head went on.

He said just what Bud told me!

But he isn't even a Christian. Why should I believe him?

Because Uncle Al kind of said it, too. Fawn's father even wrote it in his letter.

And Miguel tried to tell me.

Pray to the point of knowing, Quebi had said. But even if he wanted to—and Will still wasn't sure of that—how did a person do that? How did Quebi do that?

It isn't just the words, it's also the way they say them, Margretta had said.

Don't pray just with words. Pray from your heart, Bud had told him.

That's good, Will thought. Because if he *did* decide to pray, he didn't have any words anyway.

They sat in silence for a long time, Quebi watching the fire and Will arguing inside himself until he was almost worn out. It was then, when he was strangely fighting tears again, that a thought came to him. He was glad he hadn't gone on his pilgrimage after all. As soon as he got back to Santa Fe, he was going to tell Miguel.

He didn't share the thought with God. He couldn't do that yet.

But he didn't shut Him out, either.

✟ ⁃ ✟ ⁃ ✟

Chapter Thirteen

*I*t was dusk before Mom and Fawn and Will piled into Bud's car to head back home. As they pulled out onto the road, Fawn was still on her knees in the backseat, waving to Margretta who was staying for a while to talk with Quebi about Frog Woman.

"You know what?" Fawn said.

"No," Mom said. "But I bet we're about to find out."

"I don't think being an Indian is so bad after all."

"Quick, Will," Mom said. "Write that down, date it, and make her sign it."

Will grinned at her.

"Well, now, that's nice to see," Mom said.

"What?" Fawn said. "What did you see?"

"I saw Will smile. We don't see that too often anymore. I miss it."

Fawn gave Will's shoulder a punch. "Yeah, he's turned into a regular old grouch, but I snapped him out of it today with my surprise."

"That's it, Fawn. Take all the credit," Will said.

But he grinned at her, too. Maybe it was going to be all right—as soon as he talked to Miguel.

It was nearly dark by the time they got back to town. Will asked Mom to drop him off at Miguel's corner before she took the car over to Bud's.

"Don't stay too late," Mom said. "They're expecting more snow tonight."

Will promised, and then took off, slipping and sliding on the icy brick walk to Miguel's. Even as he knocked on the door, he could see Señora Otero through the glass, hurrying to answer. Will's heart did the funny thing it always did when he was about to be face-to-face with Miguel's beautiful mother.

But the face that greeted him wasn't wearing its usual graceful smile. It was, in fact, puffy as if she'd been crying, and there were, indeed, tears hanging on her lashes.

"Will—thank goodness!" she said. She pulled both of Will's gloved hands into hers. "Have you seen Miguel? Do you know where he is?"

Will could feel himself stiffening. "He's not here?" he said.

"No—come in—you'll freeze out there."

She drew him into the house. It was deathly still inside, not at all the way it always seemed to Will.

"He has been missing all day," Señora Otero said. "I went in early this morning to wake him up, and he was not there."

Will put his hand on his forehead, as if that would stop the fears that were already fighting to be heard inside.

"We have looked everywhere," she said. "José is still out, trying to find him." She clenched her slender hands together. "I so hoped he was with you, but I can see that you know no more than we do."

"I might," Will said. "I know one place where he might be."

"Where?" Señora Otero said.

But Will was already out the front door. He didn't stop until he reached San Miguel Mission, and even then he was still running as he flung himself inside. His lungs were burning with the cold, but he hardly noticed. He was too busy praying that Miguel would be there.

First he checked the hideaway near the outside steps, but Miguel wasn't there. A search of the church turned up nothing. Then Will charged up the steps to the balcony where the monks sang, but it, too, was vacant. He even went up to the bell tower, but there was no Miguel. Only the big, now-silent San José bell—and something else. Something that caught his eye in the far, dark corner.

Of course. It was a bundle of their food. Only when Will snatched it up did he realize that it was only half full.

"No!" Will said out loud.

His voice was still echoing in the bell tower as he tore down both sets of steps and threw himself down to look under the back pew. There was only one sleeping bag there.

A search of the statues and all the other nooks and crannies they'd made use of revealed the same thing: Will's things were still there, but Miguel's were not.

"No," Will said again, but it wasn't a convincing sound. He knew Miguel had gone on the pilgrimage without him, and his fears wouldn't go unheard this time.

You have to go after him! He's out there in the snow by himself—it's your fault—go get him!

But even before he started for the door, Will stopped and slouched heavily against the stone wall. Miguel had a 12-hour head start on him. Will couldn't catch him on foot if he were a cheetah, for Pete's sake.

"What do I do?" Will said to the empty church. "What do I do, God?"

Suddenly it was far, far too silent and too alone in the

church. It was too alone anywhere for him right now. There was only one thing to do, and that was to get help. Grown-up help.

But who? Who was going to understand?

You said you were going to do this all on your own. You told everybody. How are you gonna go back now and tell them you messed it all up?

But Miguel is out there! He's by himself in the snow! He even said it would be too hard to hike—

Why do I argue so much?!

The screaming thoughts drove Will right out the door and into the snow, which was now falling as heavy as corn flakes. The wind had picked up, too, and the snow swirled before his eyes, just as the voices were swirling in his head. He had to get to someplace where he could think again.

Before he even realized where he was going, Will headed for the hideaway spot, down on the steps at the side of the chapel. The snow still fell on him there, but he was out of the wind, where he could stop his thoughts from swirling.

All right, he told himself sternly, *you have to tell a grown-up where he is.*

There was nothing—and then only the sad little voice that said: *I wish Dad was here.*

Don't be a nincompoop! he told himself. *If Dad were here, this wouldn't have happened in the first place. Find another dad-person.*

Another "dad-person"? Where had that thought come from? What was a dad-person, anyway? A person who seemed like a dad? Like Bud—or Mr. T.—or Quebi—or Uncle Al?

The anxious thoughts all seemed to stop and stare. Will himself stared down at his knees.

I do have a lot of people who are like dads to me. Jeepers— even Mom is a better dad than some people's own fathers *are.*

And what had almost every one of them told him in one way

or another? He put his face in his hands, but the answer wouldn't go away: *You've gotta pray. You can't stop praying just because you don't get what you want right away. Pray and follow the prayer to the point of knowing.*

Will knew one thing for sure by now—*not* praying sure wasn't working. It might even be hurting some things—like Miguel.

And he'd promised Bud that when he wasn't doing fine anymore, he would think about God. He wasn't doing fine right now.

Will pulled his hands away from his face and folded them into a tight ball between his knees. Squeezing his eyes shut, he whispered, "God? I'm sorry. But will You still help me? Will You please help us find Miguel?"

He didn't hear an answer, but he did have a knowing. He had to go and tell Señora Otero where Miguel was, and then he had to get one of his dad-people to take him up to Santuario de Chimayo. He didn't let himself think about how they were going to make it up the road with the snow falling as hard as it was. One thing at a time.

Will sensed something—or someone—was looking at him. He unfolded his hands and brought his face up. Luis was staring right at him.

Will felt a spasm of fear that brought him up to his feet. Luis, however, had the element of surprise on his side, and he shoved him back down and stood over him, his gash of a smile cut into his face. The smile didn't get to his eyes, though. They were cold and empty.

"Hey," Will said. "Lemme go, would ya, Luis? I got somethin' I gotta do."

"You only got one thing to do, An-glow. You gotta pay for all the wrong you done to me."

"Look, we've been over this a thousand times," Will said. "I told the whole class about the stamp thing. I looked like the loser, not you. And it wasn't my fault you got sent to reform school. You were the one doin' the stealin', not me. Now, come on—I gotta go—"

"What about you standin' up for my little pipsqueak cousin?"

"What cousin?" Will said. "I don't know any of your relatives, Luis, and if I did I probably wouldn't stick up for 'em."

"You did. You tried to take me down for *him.*"

"Him who?"

Will was truly confused, and he didn't have time for this. With every minute that passed, Miguel was getting farther and farther away from them and further and further into the cold. He tried again to stand up, but this time Luis grabbed him by the front of his jacket and stuck his face near Will's. He had done it so many times, Will had his front teeth memorized.

"You know my cousin," Luis said. "He's your sissy friend. Miguel."

He said the name as if he'd been forced to say "Hitler." Will stared at him.

"Miguel is *not* your cousin!" he said.

"I *wish* he was not," Luis said. "He has betrayed the family by being friends with you, An-glow. You are both cowards."

"Knock it off!" Will said.

He wrenched his jacket out of Luis's grasp and gave him a shove backwards. Luis got off balance, giving Will just enough time to stand up. He pushed his nose right up against Luis's. Luis pulled back, but only a few inches.

"You can call me whatever you want!" Will shouted at him. "But don't call Miguel a coward. He's brave—braver than you'll ever be! He's as brave as his father—"

Luis cut him off with a hard laugh. "His father? His father ain't brave, he was forced into the army—"

"A lot of people were drafted!"

"And he ran away."

"You are such a liar!" Will cried. "I saw a picture of him in his uniform!"

Luis let his eyes close into slits. "Nobody seen him since the day he got that picture tooken."

Will was too stunned to answer back this time, and in the instant he paused to take it in, Luis plowed into Will's belly and hiked him up over his shoulder. He might have been shorter than Will, but he was wiry. Will kicked and pounded, but Luis held him with arms like iron clamps.

"Put me down, Luis, you liar!" Will cried as Luis carried him up the steps.

"Sure, An-glow," Luis said, and he dumped Will without ceremony, right at the feet of Pablo and Rafael.

"Hey, An-glow!" Rafael said. He wiggled his fingers down at Will and put his foot on Will's chest.

"Did he tell you where the sissy is?" Pablo said to Luis.

"No," Luis said, "but we'll just use him. He's better anyway."

Rafael gave a bark-laugh. "Better than a sissy."

"Better for what?" Will said.

Luis didn't answer. He had obviously used up his quota of words for the week and was now content to let Rafael do the talking while he and Pablo wrapped a thick rope around Will's wrists. He could still kick, but once Luis hoisted him over his shoulder again, it didn't make much difference. He could kick and scream all he wanted, but it wasn't fazing Luis.

"Shut up, will you?" Rafael said.

"Yeah, shut up," Pablo said.

"You want me to gag him, Luis?" Rafael said.

Will felt Luis nod. He clamped his mouth shut, but Pablo pried it open and shoved a rag into it. Will continued to make muffled sounds as Pablo and Rafael opened the front door of the chapel and Luis carried him inside.

What are we doing in here? Will thought. And then he

relaxed a little. *The Three Amigos probably think I'll be scared if they leave me in here with all these weird statues,* he thought. *Little do they know.*

Just to be on the safe side, Will forced himself to bug out his eyes in terror and kick with new vigor. Luis just gripped him more tightly and proceeded up the steps to the balcony.

Even better, Will thought. *They don't know how much time I've spent up here!*

But Luis didn't stop at the balcony. He made his way with his Will-load all the way up to the bell tower, where once again he dumped him. From outside, Will's head could be seen through a small window in the tower.

It's still okay, Will thought. *It's gonna get cold up here, but it's okay.*

At least it was until Pablo took hold of the bell rope, pulled Will's ankles together, and tied the rope around them.

"Guess what happens if you move your legs, An-glow?" Rafael said, eyes shimmering like it was Christmas morning.

Will glared at him. That was a cinch: The bell would ring and probably leave him deafer than a post. It was almost worth it to kick his leg right now and give all of them the headache of their lives. He was even considering it, when Luis said, "The sign."

"We got it!" Pablo said.

He reached inside his greasy jacket and pulled out a big piece of heavy paper, which he unfolded and displayed proudly. Will didn't have to force his eyes to bulge this time. They did it on their own.

I'M NOT COMIN DOWN TIL I GET $100 FOR WAR BONDS

"We're gonna put this in the window, An-glow!" Rafael said. "And people down there are gonna see the top of your head—"

"Your *stupid* head!" Pablo put in.

Will gave him a stony stare and slid down on his spine. The bell tilted nervously.

"Sit up, An-glow!" Luis said. And he took hold of the rope that was coiled around Will's wrists and wrenched him back up. The San José bell gave a sleepy first-clang, and the Three Amigos slapped their hands over their ears. Will scrunched his face up, but he could already feel the pain in his head.

"Don't move again," Luis said to him.

I'll move if I want! Will wanted to scream at him.

If Luis read it in his eyes, he didn't show it. He merely jerked his head at Pablo and Rafael and went for the steps. Rafael couldn't seem to resist a final toe-push against Will's leg. As the bell gave a weak clang that went right through Will's head, the Three Amigos tore down the steps, laughing.

✠ ⬥ ✠

Chapter Fourteen

They sound like a bunch of hyenas with rabies, Will told himself. *Good riddance!*

But the relief of having them gone lasted only about seven seconds. The Three Amigos had definitely learned some new tricks in reform school. It didn't take Will long to figure out that they had him in a fix he wasn't going to get out of easily.

With the sign hanging in the window, anybody who saw his head sticking up was just going to think he was up in the tower pulling a prank to raise money. Who was going to come up to rescue him if he didn't look like he wanted to be rescued, except maybe Mom—and what were the chances of her coming along?

If he rang the bell, of course, somebody would know something was wrong, but by the time they figured it out, his head would be ready to explode.

There *was* one glimmer of hope. The monks rang the bell every night at eight o'clock. That was how Miguel always knew when to go home, he'd said. They rang it from below, in the balcony, but if Will could scoot himself close enough to the opening in the floor they might look up and see him.

His mind started to race. *Okay—okay—if I just curve the top part of me down to the floor and move kinda like a worm, I might be able to do it without moving my legs—*

He took a deep breath and leaned sideways.

"Don't move, An-glow!" a voice shouted from below. "We are watching you!"

Go suck an egg! Will muffled into his gag. Not being able to say anything was turning out to be the worst part.

No. The worst part was knowing Miguel was somewhere in the snow alone, and nobody else knew where to go to look for him.

I must be the biggest loser in the entire world, Will thought miserably. *Why didn't I listen to anybody? Why did I stop praying? God—why did I do that? Are You even gonna help me ever again? If You don't, that's okay. I'll stay here all night, but please help Miguel! I can't stand it that I got him into this. He was doing it all for me, not his dad. His dad was a coward that ran away! He did it for me. What's my dad gonna think of me?*

The thought of Dad suddenly turned Will to stone.

I was gonna go up to Chimayo and do this big heroic mission to bring him home—and now Miguel's cold and alone—I'm cold and alone—and Dad's still cold and alone, every day in that prison camp. How does he stand it?

The answer to that was easy. Uncle Al had said it Christmas night. Rudy Hutchinson was praying.

Will began to sob into his gag then. *I musta just now followed a prayer to the point of knowing,* Will thought as he cried. Because he did know something now: Nothing worked right without God. Nothing.

His thoughts were suddenly interrupted by a voice below, coming from outside the chapel, and he strained to hear.

"Hey," said the voice. "Is that a real person or a dummy up there?"

"It is a real boy, Señor."

If Will could have gritted his teeth, he would have. It was Rafael answering in a tone so sweet he could have sprinkled it on his cereal.

"He won't come down until he's raised $100," Rafael said.

"Here. I hope this helps."

Will wasn't sure—it was a long way to the ground from where he sat, ready to explode—but he thought he heard something clanking against metal, as if coins were being dropped into a can.

I gotta be imagining it, Will told himself.

But a few minutes later, there was another voice, saying, "How long's he been up there?" and another clinking sound. This time Will knew he wasn't dreaming it up. The Three Amigos were actually collecting money down there.

Will chomped at the gag. He was sure if he didn't get to yell, "Don't fall for it! They're robbing you!" the veins in his forehead were going to burst open.

There was more clanking, and still more voices.

"I heard there was some kid pulling a crazy stunt out here," one said, "but I didn't believe it. Sure enough, there he is."

"Here you go, kids. Here's two bits for the war effort," said another.

Some of them even directed their comments right up to Will.

"You'll be down before you know it at this rate, kid!"

"Yeah, if the rats don't get you first!"

Rats?

Will twitched, and the San José bell bonged and sent a pain searing through his head.

When it stopped, Will could hear more voices below, all commenting on his "guts." There must be 20 people down there right now, standing in a snowstorm—and the Three Amigos must be collecting a small fortune.

Why can't one of 'em be somebody who knows me? Will thought as he tried to sit perfectly still. *Like Fawn. I wish I told her something about the plan.*

Or Mom.

Will groaned into the rag. Mom must be ready to tear her hair out by now. This was getting worse with every thought. There was nothing to do now *but* pray.

Send somebody, God—please. Anybody.

It may have been the quickest answer to a prayer since the loaves and fishes, for just then Will heard a voice he *did* recognize.

"You are the bad boys! Where Will? Where Will?"

It was Abe, crying out his questions at the top of his lungs. The only thing louder was a sudden shout from the crowd.

"Hey, where are they goin' with that can?" somebody cried. "I was gonna put five bucks in there!"

"Good thing you didn't, 'cause I think the rest of us just got duped!"

"Go after the little banditos!"

Go, Abe! Will wanted to shout. *Chase them down!*

Abe obviously had no such intentions, because he kept yelling, "Will! Where Will?"

"You talking about the kid up there?"

Yes! Somebody come up here!

He couldn't wait any longer. He had to get somebody up here before they all went away. Holding his breath, Will lifted his tied-up legs and swung them. The San José bell began to peal.

He kept swinging until the entire bell tower vibrated. The noise was so deafening, Will couldn't even hear his own thoughts, but he kept clanging the bell with his legs.

After what seemed like forever, the bell tower door flew open, and a red-faced monk leaped into the tiny room, robe flowing behind him, and grabbed the rope. Will rolled out of the way and right into a pair of very large feet. When he rolled to his back again, he saw Abe standing over him.

"Muffa—muffa—muff-muff-muffa muff!" Will said.

It took Abe a good five seconds to figure out that he was saying, "Pull this rag out of my mouth!"

He did. By then, the monk had the bell stopped.

Will's ears were ringing and his head was pounding. "Pick me up and carry me downstairs!" he said to Abe. "Hurry up—I'll explain on the way down!"

"Will!" Abe said gleefully. "I find you!"

"Yeah, Pal. Now come on, take me down!"

Still congratulating himself for discovering Will's whereabouts, Abe tossed Will over his shoulder like a bag of charcoal and headed down the steps. The monk called out to them, but Will spurred Abe on. There was no time for explanations right now.

He directed Abe to open the front door just a crack to see if there was still a crowd outside. There were a few angry stragglers left, but they all had their backs to the door.

"That way," Will hissed, and jerked his head toward the hideaway. For the first time that night, Will was thankful for the snow that gave them cover until they were out the door and safely concealed on the steps. Together they untied the rope; Abe was so eager to get it undone, Will thought he was going to go after it with his teeth. As they worked Will tried to formulate a new plan. He needed to have a few questions answered first.

"Abe, what are you doing out by yourself?" he said.

"Help find Will!"

"I can't believe Bud let you wander around alone, though. And Tina—yikes, she barely lets you go to the bathroom by yourself."

He stopped and narrowed his eyes at Abe. "They didn't let you, did they? You snuck out, didn't you?"

Abe put his fist up to his mouth and talked into it. "Find Will. I find Will!"

"It's okay, pal," Will said. "But I gotta get you back to Bud and I gotta tell Señora Otero where Miguel is."

Abe was nodding slowly. Will knew he had no idea what he was talking about, but he knew Abe would do whatever he told him.

"Come on," Will said. "We gotta go down DeVargas Street to a friend of mine's house. But we're gonna have to take a round-about way because I don't think the coast is clear yet."

He looked down DeVargas, in the opposite direction from Miguel's. If they went down that way, cut through a couple of yards, and doubled back, they could cross Old Santa Fe Trail farther down and not be noticed. Then they could go through some more yards to get to Miguel's.

"Follow me," Will said.

He stood up, but his legs didn't want to work. They'd been tied up for so long, they were half asleep.

"Abey do," Abe said cheerfully, and once more he tossed Will over his shoulder.

I've spent more time on people's backs tonight than I have on my own feet! he thought. And then he hung on as Abe charged down the street.

When they arrived in the alley across the street from Miguel's house, they stopped for Abe to catch his breath, hiding behind a pickup truck with a large piece of canvas thrown over the bed. Will was glad Abe had acted as packhorse. They'd made it in half the time it would have taken them if Will had been trying to run through the thick drifts of snow.

But when Will was sure there was no one lurking in the shadows and they hurried across the street, through the gate, and up to the front door, it didn't seem to make much difference how good their travel time had been. When Will knocked, no one answered. He peered in through the window but the house was empty. Even when he pounded on the door with his fists, no one came. Panic seized him like a giant pair of pliers.

I can't wait for her! What am I gonna do now? I need help. Mom—no, she only has the motorcycle. I need someone with a car. I need Bud—

"Okay, pal, we're gonna kill two birds with one stone," he said to Abe.

"Kill birds?"

"No—it's just an expression—forget it. I want you to do something for me. You gotta help, okay?"

Abe beamed and nodded.

"Run to Bud as fast as you can. Bring him back here. I'm gonna hide here by the door so I can watch for the Three—for the bad boys."

"Bad boys," Abe said darkly.

"Yeah. If you see them, just keep running. Bring Bud back here. You sure you understand?"

Abe nodded. Will made him repeat the instructions to him twice, and then he had to let him go. He couldn't lose any more time.

With Abe gone, Will was again alone in the absolute stillness of the snow. The wind had died down and the flakes had slowed, so that the Barrio felt like the inside of a church. A very *cold* church. Will huddled on the step, arms hugged around himself, and filled the silence with prayers.

He was convinced he was nearly frozen to death when he heard a door open beyond Miguel's gate. Being careful not to lean too far from the shadow, Will peered out to see who might be coming out of the house. Maybe it was Señora Otero. Maybe she'd been going door-to-door looking for Miguel—

But it was Luis Will saw emerging from the open door two houses down, with Pablo and Rafael behind him. Will looked around wildly for a better hiding place, but Luis and his friends didn't appear to be looking for *him*. Luis only gave one slanted glance over his shoulder, and then he moved like a cat up against the wall, slowly inching his way with his back to it as he clutched a bulging cloth bag. Behind him, the other two boys did the same, toting bags of their own. If Will wasn't mistaken, they were sneaking.

They don't live here in the Barrio, Will thought. *What are they up to?*

They only went as far as the pickup truck Will and Abe had hidden behind, and they lifted the canvas tarp and slipped in under it, bags and all.

And not a moment too soon, because another door opened, and a man came out, head ducked against the snow, tossed a small suitcase into the front seat of that same truck, and climbed in and drove off.

Will stood up and took a huge, relieved breath. At least that was one thing he didn't have to worry about.

But there was plenty of other stuff. Where was Abe with Bud? Why didn't Señora Otero get home—or Uncle José?

What if they're at the hospital? he thought. *What if somebody found Miguel half dead on the way to Chimayo? What if— stop it, Will! You're thinking like Neddie. Come on—you gotta pray.*

And he had to keep moving. If he stood still any longer, he was afraid he would freeze to the spot. Digging his hands deep into the pockets of his jacket, he went to the wall that surrounded the little house, stomping his feet, and paced its length. Every step beat out a rhythm—like the Indians: *Help, God. Please help.*

But the rhythm was broken when suddenly, from the wall above him, something dropped on him and knocked him down into the snow. The something was alive.

✝ • ✝ • ✝

Chapter Fifteen

*W*ill fell face first into the snow with the person on his back, but even from that position he knew it was Fawn. She had jumped him so many times, he'd have known her wiry arms and sturdy legs anywhere.

Cheeks aching with cold, Will struggled out from under her and shoved her away. She was already coming back after him before she even hit the ground.

"What are you doin', Fawn!" he said.

"That's what I'd like to know about *you!*" she said. She stood up, hands on hips, glaring down at him. "What are you up to, running around at night in the snow?" Her eyes narrowed. "You better not be having an adventure without me."

"This is no adventure, believe me," Will said. He got to his feet and brushed the snow from his now snow-coated dungarees. The rolled-up cuffs were heavy with it, and he went after those next. "Did you sneak out, too?"

"Yeah—when Abe told me you were here! When you didn't come home on time, Mom came here right away, but there was nobody here then. Still, when Abe said—"

Will stopped pulling snow out of his cuffs and stared at her. "Abe told you?"

"Yeah. He came back to the house, and Mom and Bud were both out looking for you, so he told me."

"He was supposed to tell Bud! I need for Bud to come with the car!"

"I told you, Bud wasn't there—"

"Did you leave him a note or anything?"

"No—I wouldn't tell on you, Will."

"Tell on me?" Will rolled his eyes. "I *told* Abe to tell Bud. I need him!"

"For what?"

Will didn't answer, because just then a car engine roared from the corner, sounding as if it were about to take its last breath.

"Bud!" Will said.

He hiked himself up onto the wall to see, but it wasn't Bud's old Chevy. It was a nearly as ancient pickup truck with a sand-pitted windshield, and a whiskered driver who looked through it out of a long, weathered face.

"It's Uncle José!" Will said.

"Uncle who?" Fawn said. "Swell. One *more* thing you haven't told me—"

Will ignored her and scrambled down to meet José as he pulled the truck up outside the wall and unfolded his tall self from the driver's seat. The passenger door opened, too, and Señora Otero hurried up to Will.

"Who *are* these people?" Fawn said.

"Will—any word?" the señora said.

Will's heart sank. The anxiety was still etched in her beautiful face. He shook his head.

"We thought for certain we would find him at San Miguel

Mission," she said. "Someone told us my nephews were seen there. They cannot leave Miguel alone for a moment, but they were gone, too."

Will swallowed hard. "Miguel hasn't been there since early this morning. I was supposed to meet him there and we were gonna go up to the Santuario—"

Señora Otero's eyebrows lifted. "Santuario?"

"At Chimayo," Will said. The words hurt as they came out. They were the hardest ones he'd ever had to say.

"I do not understand."

"Me neither," Fawn said.

"There's not time to explain!" Will said. "He went on up there by himself because his stuff was gone from the church when I went there."

"What stuff?" Fawn said.

Will wanted to belt her one. "Our supplies and sleeping bags—"

"Sleeping bags?" Fawn said.

Her voice had by now risen to a screech, but this time it was Señora Otero who silenced her.

"José—" she said sharply. The rest came out in Spanish, but Will could tell by her pointing—and the way Uncle José turned immediately to the truck—that he was to go after Miguel.

"I have to go with him," Will said, " 'cause this is all my fault."

As he went for the truck, he knew Fawn was right on his heels.

"You're not going without me again," she said.

I know Fawn's not gonna like what I'm about to do, but I don't know any other way, Will thought, and then he nodded.

"And you're gonna have a lot of explaining to do on the way," Fawn said.

"Sure," Will said, and he hoisted himself onto the truck's front seat.

But as she tried to climb up next to him, Will gave a mighty heave with his forearm and sent her reeling backwards into the snow.

"Go, Uncle José!" he cried as he slammed the door.

The truck wheezed to life, and Will got the window down and leaned out.

"Go home and tell Mom we're going to the Santuario de Chimayo!" he shouted to her. "Tell her!"

Fawn got to her feet already waving her fists. The Christmas boots were stomping the ground as the truck rounded the corner to Old Santa Fe Trail.

Will leaned back, a spring poking him in the spinal column, and squeezed his eyes shut. *God, please get her to tell Mom, no matter how mad she is at me. Please.*

He opened his eyes and stared miserably out the foggy side window. Could he really expect God to answer any of his prayers after the way he'd ignored Him for so long? Maybe He'd do it for Miguel, who had never stopped praying. Or for Mom, so she wouldn't worry. Or for Señora Otero and Uncle José—

He tightened his eyes again. *I've hurt so many people trying to do this on my own. God's never gonna answer a prayer of mine again!*

"Mi amigo," Uncle José said.

Will's head jerked toward him in surprise. The old man pointed a long, thick finger at the dashboard. For the first time, Will saw a figure attached there. It was one of Uncle José's santos.

"I don't mean to be rude or anything," Will said, "but in my church, we don't pray to saints."

"Jesucristo," Uncle José said.

Saint Hay-su Crisco? Will thought. *I never heard of that one.*

Uncle José pointed again, more insistently this time, and Will reluctantly leaned forward to inspect the santo more closely. He knew at once who it was.

"Jesus?" Will said.

Uncle José nodded and with a deep sigh focused on the road. Will looked again at the little statue.

Although the face of this Jesus was as Spanish as Miguel himself, there was no mistaking the look in his eyes. There was love there, love that loved even when His people thought He couldn't help them, and when they'd messed things up so badly there didn't seem to be any way to fix them. The love in that face seemed so real, it was like Miguel had told him—it was as if Uncle José had breathed his faith into the wooden face—right from the love Jesus had given him.

Will blinked. *The statue isn't Jesus,* he told himself.

But as he gazed at it, he couldn't help thinking about the real Jesus, the real God—the one who did love him.

"Uncle José?" he said. "Do you think God'll still help us even though I messed this whole thing up and it's my fault that Miguel's out there in the cold by himself—"

Uncle José was already nodding. Will sighed, and he began to pray.

He prayed as they wound through Santa Fe and out onto the empty, lonely road that he and Miguel had planned to take. He prayed with his eyes glued to the window, the truck moving at a crawl so he and Uncle José could search. The clouds had cleared and there was no wind, so their eyes could see far across the vast land in the moonlight. The snow on the ground glowed as if there were a light beneath it, but they didn't see a sign of Miguel. Will barely allowed himself to blink for fear of missing him, and his eyes burned.

"Santa Cruz," Uncle José said, nodding out the window at a cluster of sleeping adobes.

"This is the last town before Chimayo!" Will said. "Maybe he made it all the way to the church! Maybe he isn't out there freezing somewhere—do you think?"

Uncle José didn't answer. He pulled the truck to a stop in front of one of the squatty adobe houses and opened the car door.

"What are you doing?" Will said. "We can't stop until we find him—"

But Uncle José closed the door behind him, and Will watched him walk up to the house and knock on the door.

He's gonna ask somebody for help, Will thought. *I shoulda thought of that myself. I shoulda thought of that a long time ago.*

He looked at the loving face of the statue and closed his eyes to pray again.

Before long there was a tap on the glass, and Will rolled the window down. A Spanish woman wrapped in a blanket peered in at him as Uncle José climbed back into the truck.

"Boy pass heer," she said. Her English was as broken as her front teeth, and Will had to strain to understand her. "Day—in the day."

"Before dark?" Will said.

She bobbed her head. "*Si.* Many—" she searched for the word and then seemed to give up and instead bent over as if she were carrying a heavy load on her back.

"He was still carrying all his stuff," Will said. "Was he okay?"

She frowned and shrugged.

"Sick?" Will said. Why, he wondered, hadn't he ever bothered to learn Spanish? "Hurt?" he said.

He curled up his hand and whimpered like a puppy. Her eyes lit up.

"Si!" she said. She took a few steps as if she were limping.

"Gracias, Juanita," Uncle José said.

The woman stepped back, still bobbing her head and pretending to limp.

Will sat straight up in the seat, hands clutching the dashboard. "He got this far before dark," he said. "He was strong enough to carry his stuff—he couldn'ta been hurt that bad. Maybe he was just tired. Don't you think he was just tired?"

Uncle José didn't answer, but from the way he pressed his foot down hard on the gas pedal, Will knew he didn't think that at all. Will didn't ask any more questions, and the only prayer he could get out was *Please, God, please.*

This wasn't the endless expanse of land they'd passed through up to this point. Here, the side of the road dropped off sharply as the ground dipped into a wide gully before sloping upwards into the foothills. There was hill after rocky hill—for Miguel to be lost in.

"I'm sure he would have stayed on the road," he said. "That's what we planned—"

"*Cuidado!*" Uncle José cried suddenly.

Will whipped around to see Uncle José pointing off to the left. At first Will didn't see what he was looking at, and he slid closer and craned his neck. Uncle José stopped the truck right in the road and wound down his window.

Then Will saw it—a lopsided little tent pitched beside the road like a forlorn stranger at the foot of a rocky, snowy hillside.

"That's Miguel's!" Will cried. He flung open the truck door and hit the ground already running. Both feet flew out from under him, and he was on his back staring at the snow as it fell, unhindered, into his face. He rolled over onto his hands and knees and crawled across the road, then stood up and felt his way down a slope of rocks. When his feet found thick snow, he ran for the tent, screaming Miguel's name as he went.

There was no answer from inside the flaps. Back on hands and knees again, Will threw the flaps back and crawled into the tent. His hands immediately found a small mound in the dark that he could only hope was his friend.

"Miguel!" he said. "It's Will. Wake up, Miguel!"

The mound stirred. Will put his face close to it and felt soft breath on his cheek. He felt around with his gloved hands—it was a face, all right.

Will reached behind him and smacked the tent flaps open again. Then he lifted the face he held in his hands toward the opening. In the moonlight, he could see that it was Miguel, with his eyes closed.

"Uncle José!" Will shouted. "He's here!" He closed the flaps and pulled Miguel's face up close to his own. "Wake up, Miguel. We're here—me and Uncle José. We're gonna take you home where it's warm."

It was dry inside the tent, but that was the only thing that could be said for its conditions. It was as dark and cold as Will's basement, and a lot more cramped, what with all of Miguel's packages piled inside.

What were we thinking, planning to carry all that stuff? Will thought. He got close to Miguel's face again. "Miguel!" he said. "Open your eyes!"

Slowly, the big black eyes fluttered open, and a tiny gleam crept into them.

"Weel," Miguel said. "You came."

The breath was stronger in Will's nose as Miguel talked, and something about it wasn't right. That, and the heat that seemed to steam from Miguel like the Hutchinsons' radiator.

Heat? Will thought. *In this cold tent?* He ripped off his glove and pressed his bare hand on the forehead that peeked out from Miguel's jacket hood. It burned against his palm.

Will's heart went straight to his throat, and once again he whipped open a tent flap.

"Uncle José!" he cried out. "Miguel's got a fever! Hurry!"

He could see Uncle José just picking his way down the rocks at the side of the road. The old man stopped and cupped his hand around his ear.

"Fever!" Will shouted.

At once, Uncle José turned around and went back up the rocks like a mountain goat, back toward the truck which he had pulled to the side of the road.

"No—come quick!" Will cried. But Uncle José climbed inside and started it up without even closing his door.

"Maybe he's going to get a doctor," Will said to Miguel.

Outside the tires squealed and Will looked out again to see the truck lurch backward. But then the wheels turned and headed it for the rocky drop below.

"You can't drive the truck down here!" Will shouted. "Uncle José, no!"

The truck continued on, its nose straight downward as Uncle José guided it over the rocks. It rocked first to one side, then to the other as it crept.

And then one wheel hit a pointed rock and bounced off. The whole truck swayed and then slid, bouncing and jouncing down the hill sideways. When it hit the final boulder at the bottom, it was airborne once again. Will watched in horror as it twisted upside down and landed with a crash on its top.

✢ ✢ ✢

Chapter Sixteen

*A*w, man—I don't believe this!"

"What is it, Weel?" Miguel said.

His voice was thready, and his eyebrows struggled to knit together. Will could feel his own panic rising. *I can't go nutso on him, God,* he prayed. *Please, You gotta help me.*

He took a huge breath and leaned close to Miguel. "Uncle José musta thought he was drivin' a tank," he said. "I'm gonna go see if he's okay, and then I'll be right back. Keep your eyes open, all right?"

Miguel nodded but promptly closed his eyes with a sigh. Still fighting down his fear, Will bolted from the tent and took off for the truck. *I'm* not *doing fine, God,* he thought. *Please, please, please—*

So far God didn't seem to be answering. Uncle José's head and shoulders were hanging out of the window, resting on the snow, and a trail of blood was making its way down from a cut on his forehead. He was breathing, but his eyes were closed.

"Uncle José!" Will said.

There was no answer.

"Wake up!"

Not even a groan. Will put his own forehead down on the snow and struggled against tears. *What am I gonna do now, God? I don't know what to do!*

God was as silent as Uncle José, but the cold of the snow on Will's forehead was somehow calming. Slowly he began to think straight thoughts.

"All right," he said, though he was pretty sure Uncle José couldn't hear him. "I'm gonna go get Miguel and bring him up here. Then at least I got both of you together. Yeah, that's what I'm gonna do. Don't go away."

Uncle José reassured him with his silence. Forcing himself not to run like a terrified chicken, Will made his way back to the little tent, praying all the way that Miguel would still be awake.

He wasn't, but it only took one shake to bring him back around, and this time he even tried to smile.

"You wanna go for a ride?" Will said to him.

"In the truck?" Miguel said.

"Nope. On me. Everybody's been cartin' me around on their backs all night. I figure it's my turn to cart somebody else—and you're it."

He was trying to keep his voice out of the tears-zone. He wasn't sure if it was helping Miguel much, but it was sure helping him. He even managed a chuckle as he pulled the blankets tighter around Miguel.

"I'm wrappin' you up like a burrito," he said. "And then I'm gonna sling you over my back and haul you up to the truck." He kept talking as he followed his own instructions. "We can't get in the truck 'cause right now it's upside down, but if we get up close next to it, we'll be outa the wind, just like in our hideaway."

"Upside down?" Miguel said faintly.

"Yeah, wait'll you see it. Even Neddie couldn'ta dreamed up something like this."

"Wait until we tell him," Miguel said.

I just hope we get the chance, Will thought. But he forced out a laugh as he started the trek across the snow toward the overturned truck with Miguel on his back. On the way, he kept talking, putting ideas into words as they came into his head.

"Once I get the tent up there and get you settled in," he said, "I'm gonna make some farolitos out of our grocery bags and the candles we brought and put 'em up by the road so maybe somebody'll stop and help us."

"Farolitos," Miguel said.

"Yeah, and then I'm gonna make a little fire—not too big—Quebi makes his fire real small. And I'm gonna heat up some snow and wash off Uncle José's cut. We bought a little bean pot, didn't we?"

Miguel mumbled an answer Will didn't really listen to. He just kept talking, just kept working, just kept praying. His chest was still pumping out fear, but at least Miguel didn't seem to know it. Once Will had his tent back up, attached on one side to the truck, Miguel snuggled into his sleeping bag as if he were home in bed.

Will tried not to think about the sweet smell of Miguel's hot breath as he made him some bouillon on the fire and spooned it into his mouth.

He tried not to notice how cold Uncle José's skin had gotten as he bathed his cut with warmed-up snow.

And he tried not to look too many times up at the road where three faintly flickering farolitos he had set up signaled the presence of the three of them below the rocks. The sight of that barren, carless road made him want to panic again.

Instead, he kept his attention on Miguel. When the big eyes dropped closed again, Will shook his arm.

"Stay awake, Miguel," he said.

"I am awake," he said. "I am praying."

"Oh," Will said. "Well, pray out loud, would ya? I wanna hear it, too. I don't think God's listening to me."

Miguel's eyes startled open. "You are praying, Weel? I thought you did not believe—"

"I started again, okay? But I don't think it's working."

"It is working," Miguel said. "You are here."

Yeah, well, if it weren't for me you wouldn't need *me here,* Will thought.

Miguel, however, didn't mention that at all as he whispered his prayers to God. All he could seem to do was thank Him that Uncle José was still alive and that Will had come to rescue him and that Will was so smart, he knew just what to do. It was making Will feel worse, not better. Finally, he said, "You better stop now, Miguel. God's not gonna believe any of that stuff."

Miguel's eyebrows came together. "I do not understand."

"It's all my fault we're in this mess—don't you get it? If I'd prayed in the first place, I woulda figured out it was stupid for us to try to go on this mission by ourselves. And then I didn't tell my mom the truth when we left for the pueblo this morning. If I had, she woulda let me come tell you I couldn't go and then you wouldn't of started off by yourself and gotten hurt—"

"It was not your fault I was hurt," Miguel said.

"Yes, it was—"

"It was Luis."

Will stared down at him. "Luis? What's he got to do with it?"

Miguel licked his lips. "The three of them were on the streets when I left San Miguel Mission."

"At that hour?" Will said. "Don't they ever sleep?"

"I think they had not yet gone to bed."

"What did they do to you?" Will said. He wasn't sure he wanted to know. This was getting worse by the minute.

"They saw me and I ran from them and into the hideaway, but they found me there. Our secret place is not a secret anymore."

"Yeah, I know."

"I ran some more. I almost ran back to my house, but I had the pack on my back, and my mama would have asked questions."

"You should have, Miguel! Don't ever listen to me again, okay?"

Miguel looked as if he were having trouble keeping his eyes open, but he managed to shake his head. "I did listen to you, Weel. I listened to your voice in my head. You were saying, 'You are not puny, Miguel. You can be brave like your father.' "

Will felt a pang, and he turned his eyes away. If what Luis had told him about Miguel's father was true, he didn't want Miguel to see it in his face.

"So I ran back into the mission," Miguel said. "And I bolted the door behind me. They were standing outside, shouting things at me, and I ran up to the bell tower."

Will's mind was reeling. "I don't get it. If you hid up there, how did you—"

"I dropped cans of beans on them." Miguel's mouth trembled into a smile. "I hit Pablo on the top of the head, but it did not hurt him. His head is too hard. I hit Rafael on the shoulder. He yelled something bad at me."

"I bet he did! What about Luis?"

Miguel grunted as his eyes drifted closed again. "I missed him. But the can broke and beans splashed on him. He was the most mad of all!"

"So how did you get out?" Will said.

Miguel had to lick his lips again before he could answer. "When Luis looked up to shout bad things at me, I had opened the last can of beans, and I poured it in his face." Miguel sighed.

"Then I went out the back door."

"There's a back door?"

"Only the monks may use it. I did not think they would mind. Only—it was still dark and I did not know my way back there. I tripped and fell."

"You hurt your leg before you even left Santa Fe?" Will said. "Miguel, why did you even go?"

"I was looking for you. I thought they kept you from coming to the church. I knew how much you wanted to go. I thought you went on."

"You see?" Will said. "It *was* my fault! This is all because of me. Everybody was right, Miguel—I shoulda listened. I thought I could do this big thing on my own—and I can't. Don't be friends with me, Miguel. All I'll do is get you in trouble. Okay, Miguel? Miguel?"

There was no answer. Will leaned close to the boy's face. His breath was still thick and soft, but his eyes stayed closed. Will looked frantically from him to Uncle José. Their silence screamed at him—*You should have listened! You should have listened to Bud and Uncle Al and Mr. T. and Mom. You should have listened to God!*

Even now he strained to hear Him. But it wasn't God he heard—it was a motor, chugging from far down the road, toiling to make its way up.

Will struggled to his feet, which were now so cold he could barely stand on them. There was no way they were going to take him up the slope of rocks to the roadside. There were only the farolitos, flickering pitifully in their bags, to let the driver know.

"Please God," Will said. "Please let it be Bud."

But as it drew closer, Will knew it wasn't the old Chevy. Even it wouldn't have to work so hard to climb the hill. This motor sounded more like—more like—

"Mom!" Will shouted.

Below him, Miguel stirred, but Will left him behind as he got himself halfway up the rock slope on frozen feet and waved his arms.

"Mom! Mom—we're down here!"

She couldn't possibly have seen him from the motorcycle, but it stopped just above and within seconds he saw her, peering over the edge—and beside it, the beautiful, frightened face of Señora Otero.

"We're down here—we're all down here!" Will cried. Actually, he sobbed, but he didn't try to hold it back anymore. When Mom managed to pick her way down to him, he sobbed some more, right in her arms.

It took some doing to get everyone to a warm, sheltered place. Just as Mom was starting off to Chimayo on the motorcycle to get help, Bud appeared in the Chevy, with a fuming Fawn in the front seat with him. Mom got her to put her anger on a back burner while she helped get Miguel to Bud's car; Bud and Señora Otero would take him on to Chimayo to a doctor and send someone back for Uncle José. The old man was coming around by the time an entire posse of Spanish men arrived and pulled him out of his truck. They loaded him into one car and headed for Chimayo, while Mom, Will, and Fawn piled into the back of someone else's truck with the motorcycle and followed.

They all gathered in a low, flat-roofed building where a grizzled old doctor, whom Señora Otero seemed to trust completely, tended to Miguel and Uncle José by the light of a pierced tin candelabra. A bevy of women draped in rebozos and chattering in Spanish to Señora Otero brought in hot soup and coffee and wrapped Will and Mom and the señora in blankets softer than anything Will had ever felt.

"Ortega blankets," Señora Otero said as she gave the women grateful nods.

Will didn't care if they were *Okinawa* blankets; he just

wanted to know if Miguel and Uncle José were going to be all
right. The old doctor seemed to take forever before he'd say a
word, and even then all he did was nod at Señora Otero.

Will couldn't stand it any longer.

"Are they gonna be okay?" he said. "I gotta know, 'cause this
is all my fault—"

"Miguel's fever has broken," Señora Otero said. "He is deli-
cate, like his father was. The cold and going without food were
too much for him—and the pain. But his ankle is only bruised.
It will heal quickly." She took Will's hand and squeezed it—
squeezing all the blood right to his embarrassed face, he was
sure. "You got to him just in time, and you took good care of
him. He will be fine."

"What about Uncle José?" Fawn said. She'd been there a good
hour—long enough to adopt Miguel's relatives as her own. Will,
after all, wasn't going to be involved in anything that didn't include her.

"He has a nasty cut," Señora Otero said.

"Not to mention a terrible headache, I'd guess," Mom said.

"But he's all right?" Will said. "He'll be able to make santos
again?"

"What's a santos?" Fawn said.

"Yes," Señora Otero said. "He will be fine. It would take
something much worse than this to stop him from his work."
She smiled her graceful smile at Will. "Be at peace, my friend.
All is well."

Fawn tugged at the señora's blanket. "Would somebody tell
me what a santos is?"

As Señora Otero pulled Fawn close to her, Will sank his face
into his hands.

"Everyone is going to be fine, Son," Mom said.

"No thanks to me."

"I don't understand why you think this is all your fault."

Mom lifted his chin with her fingers. "Suppose you tell me, huh?"

Will pulled his face away. He didn't want to see her face change as he told her all about the mess he'd made. But he did pour it out. He couldn't carry it around by himself anymore.

"It was a stupid idea, thinking a mission to the santuario was gonna change anything," he said as he wound up the story.

"I think a whole lot has changed," Mom said. "You've gone back to talking to God."

"Yeah," Will said. "But I shoulda figured that out before. Everybody tried to tell me—you and Bud and Mr. T. and Uncle Al. I didn't have to go to some church in Chimayo to find it out."

To his surprise, Mom gave a soft laugh. "Maybe you did, Will," she said. "Because that's where you are."

"Huh?" Will said.

Mom pointed to the far wall, and Will looked up. What appeared to be a draped altar stood in the shadows, and above it hung a cross. To one side, a pair of curtains had been pulled back to reveal a small statue of a little boy. It was wearing a pair of brand-new shoes.

"Santo Niño Perdido?" Will said.

"Who?" Fawn said. "Why don't I know what anybody's talking about anymore?"

"I'm in the Santuario de Chimayo?" Will said.

Fawn sighed. "Now I'm *really* lost!"

"But Will is not," Señora Otero said. "The lost child has been found."

She smiled at him, and this time Will didn't blush. He was too busy thinking, *Jeepers. Thanks, God.*

✝ ✝ ✝

Chapter Seventeen

*A*fter they returned to Santa Fe, Will was relieved that God was answering his prayers: Miguel and Uncle José were going to be all right. Just to make sure, he went to their house every day after school and gave Señora Otero a break, serving the two patients the supper Mom cooked for them and washing up the dishes, something Mom told Señora Otero he only did at home if she threatened him with being grounded for the rest of his life.

Actually, that was one good thing Will hadn't even asked for—the fact that Mom and Miguel's mother were becoming good friends. And Fawn seemed to like hanging out with Uncle José, probably, Will decided, because he reminded her of Quebi. He couldn't know for sure, however, because he was getting what Mom called "the cold shoulder" from Fawn.

"Cold?" Will said. "It's a Popsicle!"

"Give her some time," Mom told him. "First Emiko leaves and then you shut her out of things in your life. That's a lot for her to take at one time."

It wasn't long, however, before things started to shape up. It started the next Saturday afternoon when Mom, Fawn, and Will were out in their front yard building a snowman and Bud drove up in the Chevy with news.

"I just got off the phone with Mr. Tarantino," Bud told them. "He's gotten word that our three banditos have been picked up down near Albuquerque and they're on their way back to reform school."

"For running away?" Mom said.

Bud shook his head. "No, for burglarizing several houses in the Barrio. Apparently they used the money they raised from their little bell tower stunt to finance their trip—when they weren't stowing away in the backs of people's pickups. But the police finally caught up with them." Bud shook his head again. "They chose the wrong kid to bully down in Albuquerque—the son of the chief of police."

"It's hard to believe they're really related to Miguel," Fawn said.

"Yeah," Will said. "But he doesn't claim them too much."

That was something he'd found out during one of his long talks with Miguel while he was feeding him supper and catching him up on what he was missing in school. He'd also found out about Miguel's father.

"I thought Luis was lying to me about you guys being cousins," Will said to him that evening.

"No," Miguel said. "I am sad to say, he was telling the truth."

Will circled the spoon around Miguel's soup bowl a few times before he said, "Was he telling the truth about your father?"

Miguel's face darkened. "If he said anything bad about Papa, it was a lie!"

"So—he didn't run away right after he got his uniform and had his picture taken?"

Miguel didn't even have to answer. Will could see the anger in his eyes.

"I didn't really believe it could be true," Will said quickly. "So he must be with my dad, in Bataan, in the camp!"

Miguel turned away from the spoonful of soup Will offered him. "No," he said toward the wall. "He was never in the camp. He was killed at once when they were captured by the Japanese."

Will let the spoon clink back into the bowl. "He's dead?" he said.

"Three years. But please do not say it around Mama. It is too hard for her to speak of it."

"Your father's *dead?*" Will said. "I—I'm sorry to hear that."

"Yes . . . I didn't know how to tell you," Miguel said.

"But how come you still believe in God and still pray? How come you can even smile or anything?"

As soon as the words were out of his mouth, Will wished he could suck them all back in. *What am I doing? This is only gonna make him feel worse. I wouldn't want somebody badgerin' me with questions—*

But Miguel had turned his head toward Will again and was looking at him with large, honest eyes. For once, his eyebrows were smooth. All he said was, "What else can I do?"

Will thought about that a lot over the next several days. He thought about it when he realized that with the Three Amigos gone, nobody at school was much interested in whether Will had come up with the $500 or not. He thought about it when he and Miguel got an A on their presentation about early Indian religious beliefs, and when he told Bud later that day over a celebration soda at the Plaza Café that after learning all that they did, he decided he respected the Indians' right to worship the way they wanted to, but that he was glad he was a Christian.

Bud didn't say, "I told you so." He only said, "What makes you say that?"

Will carefully considered his chocolate malt as he put his thoughts together. "It's some of what you said. And it's a little of what Mr. T. told me. And I guess there's a lot of what Uncle Al was tryin' to say, too, and Mom." Will took a deep breath. "But most of it was Miguel. He just said something like—what else can you do? I figure I might not always be able to find you or Mr. T. or Uncle Al, but I can always find Jesus." He fidgeted with his straw. "Besides, Jesus forgives—and I need a lot of that."

Bud was quiet for a minute. Then he chuckled and said, "Will, my friend, who among us does not?"

It was a while before Miguel was able to come back to school, and Will missed him. But he didn't have to be friendless in the cafeteria for long. On Valentine's Day, Neddie got so many frilly, mushy cards from his bevy of girls, he fled from them like a rosy-cheeked kid from a gang of cheek-pinching old ladies, as Will saw it. Neddie started eating lunch with Will again, and Will decided not to give him a hard time about his absence. He did apologize for the wrecking ball comment though, and he started to tell Neddie about an idea he was cooking up.

Neddie, however, held up both hands. "I don't know about your ideas, Will," he said. "Your last one got Miguel pneumonia and a broken leg!"

"He caught a bad cold and bruised his ankle," Will said, trying not to roll his eyes.

"That's bad enough! Next time it *could* be pneumonia, or bronchitis, or streptococcus, or—"

"It's not gonna involve any diseases!" Will said. "Now do you want to hear my idea or not?"

As it turned out, Fawn was a lot more interested in the details of his plan than Neddie was. In fact, once Will told her about it, her cold shoulder thawed and Will was pretty sure all was forgiven.

After they—Will and Fawn and Miguel and Abe—had worked

on the plan together, they asked Mom and Bud to meet them at Miguel's house. No more hiding things from parents, Will told the others as they rehearsed. Abe was all for that. Even he had figured out that it now practically took an act of Congress for Tina to let him out of her sight since the night he'd wandered around Santa Fe in the snow looking for Will.

The next evening they had the parents all together at Miguel's, with Señora Otero serving her homemade salsa with cheese and bread. Abe sang in his surprisingly Bing Crosbylike voice, accompanied by Miguel, who also played a solo; Fawn recited and acted out a monologue from *Laughing Boy*; and they all sang "Over There," complete with kick line. Abe wasn't the best at that, but the parents gave them a standing ovation.

"So," Will said when they were finished and breathless, "do you think we can raise some money for bonds if we put together a show like this?"

The parents looked a little stunned.

"Will," Mom said, "you're not feeling like you have to make up for the money those boys conned people out of when they had you up in the bell tower, do you? That wasn't your fault."

"No," Will said. "This is more like us wanting to do something good for a change, something that doesn't cause a whole bunch of trouble."

Fawn gave him a hard poke in the ribs. *"Us?"* she said.

"Well, no—me. These guys are just helping me."

But Miguel was shaking his head. "We have all lost our fathers in some way," he said. "We want to do something they would be proud of."

Señora Otero was wiping her eyes. "You already have," she said.

"I don't feel like we have," Will said. "So—what do you think about a show?"

Nobody said anything for a minute or two, and Will had the

sinking feeling they were all trying to come up with a way to tell them to forget it without hurting their feelings. And then Bud spoke up.

"I personally think it's a great idea," he said. "There wasn't a dry eye in the house at the Christmas pageant, so why shouldn't you be able to knock their socks off again?"

"Bud, are you serious?" Tina said. She was already slipping her arm around Abe's shoulders as if to shield him from thrown rotten tomatoes.

"Serious as a heart attack. You kids can use the church hall and maybe we can get some of the other kids involved—you're going to need publicity, costumes, props, a set—"

"Neddie'll help us, too," Will said.

Bud's pudgy cheeks were getting pink. "I bet you could get Mr. Tarantino to let you spread the word at school. He might even lend us some of those stage lights he has stored in the auditorium."

"Lights!" Fawn's eyes sparkled as if they were in the spotlight already.

"Hmm," Mom said. "Tina, what do you think about a little bake sale to go with the show? People like to munch at the theater."

"You read my mind," Tina said. "I know a couple of the women at church who might give us part of their sugar ration for the cause—"

Tina and Mom immediately launched into a deep discussion of delectable delights. Bud got out pencil and paper and started a to-do list. Señora Otero pulled out some of her poetry to see if Fawn might like to recite it in the show. Miguel went to work with Abe at once on some new songs. And Will—

Will watched them for a minute as their faces glowed in the goldness of the light from the tin oil lamps. There was something too much about it, something that was welling up in his throat and threatening to come out as tears. Without bothering to grab his jacket, he slipped out the front door.

He had to wade through the snow to the wall, kicking out white powder ahead of him as he went, arms hugged around his middle. His dungarees were cold all the way up to his knees by the time he reached the wall, but he hiked himself on top and tilted his head backward so the tears would go back where they belonged.

Why am I about to start bawlin' like a baby? he thought. *Just about everything's okay now. I should be happy. What's wrong with me, God?*

He didn't even have to wait for God to answer. It was pretty obvious what was wrong. How could he be completely happy, ready to throw himself into their show, into life without the Three Amigos, into being friends with Fawn again, and into getting to go to the pueblo some more—how could he when Dad was still so far away—when he didn't know if he would ever come home? How did Miguel do it, knowing *his* father would *never* be with him again?

And then he remembered how.

I betcha Dad's doin' it right now, he thought. *I betcha he* knows *he's gonna see me again. I betcha God's already told him.*

"What else can I do?" Will said out loud to the silent snow.

And then he bowed his head—just like he knew Dad was doing. It might not change anything, but he had one point of knowing—the praying was going to change *him*. After all, it already had.

✢ ✦ ✢

There's More Adventure in the
CHRISTIAN HERITAGE SERIES!

The Salem Years, 1689–1691

The Rescue #1   *The Accused* #4
The Stowaway #2   *The Samaritan* #5
The Guardian #3   *The Secret* #6

The Williamsburg Years, 1780–1781

The Rebel #1   *The Prisoner* #4
The Thief #2   *The Invasion* #5
The Burden #3   *The Battle* #6

The Charleston Years, 1860–1861

The Misfit #1   *The Trap* #4
The Ally #2   *The Hostage* #5
The Threat #3   *The Escape* #6

The Chicago Years, 1928–1929

The Trick #1   *The Stunt* #4
The Chase #2   *The Caper* #5
The Capture #3   *The Pursuit* #6

The Santa Fe Years, 1944–1945

The Discovery #1   *The Stand* #3
The Mirage #2   *The Mission* #4

FOCUS ON THE FAMILY®

Like this book?

Then you'll love *Clubhouse* magazine! It's written for kids just like you, and it's loaded with great stories, interesting articles, puzzles, games, and fun things for you to do. Some issues include posters, too! With your parents' permission, we'll even send you a complimentary copy.

Simply write to Focus on the Family, Colorado Springs, CO 80995 (in Canada, write P.O. 9800, Stn. Terminal, Vancouver, B.C. V6B 4G3) and mention that you saw this offer in the back of this book. Or, call 1-800-A-FAMILY (in Canada, call 1-800-661-9800).

You may also visit our Web site (www.family.org) to learn more about the ministry or find out if there is a Focus on the Family office in your country.

• • •

"Adventures in Odyssey" is a fantastic series of books, videos, and radio dramas that's fun for the entire family—parents, too! You'll love the twists and turns found in the novels, as well as the excitement packed into every video. And the 30 albums of radio dramas (available on audiocassette or compact disc) are great to listen to in the car, after dinner . . . even at bedtime! You can hear "Adventures in Odyssey" on the radio, too. Call Focus on the Family for a listing of local stations airing these programs or to request any of the "Adventures in Odyssey" resources. They're also available at Christian bookstores everywhere.

Focus on the Family is an organization that is dedicated to helping you and your family establish lasting, loving relationships with each other and the Lord. It's why we exist! If we can assist you or your family in any way, please feel free to contact us. We'd love to hear from you!

More Great Resources
From Focus on the Family®

KidWitness Tales
New from Heritage Builders, a ministry of Focus on the Family, these action-packed tales follow fictional Bible-era kids who meet real Bible characters from the Old and New Testaments. Recommended for ages 8 and up.

The Worst Wish
Seth, the son of Jairus, thinks his sister, Tabitha, is the biggest pest! She won't leave him and his friends alone. She tattles on them and makes them look bad when they memorize Scripture. Seth's friends finally give him an ultimatum: prove to us that we're more important to you than your sister or that's the end of the friendship. Seth wishes his sister would die, but when she does, he is devastated. He knows her death is all his fault! As he pours out his sorrow to God, he realizes the importance of family relationships.

Trouble Times Ten
Ben is afraid of almost everything—especially water. Now, Israel is rejoicing in the appearance of Moses, who has said he will free them from Egypt. But instead of freedom, plague after plague comes to the land, intensifying Ben's fears. When Israel is finally released, Ben discovers he must pass through two walls of water. Just as he makes it through, he sees a child who is in danger of drowning. Ben realizes it's time to face his fear of water and learn to trust God.

Ruled Out
Ethan is tired of rules. Not only must he follow his father's strict household rules and the rules about Passover and manna—but now Moses is going up to Mount Sinai to get even more rules from God! To make things worse, Ethan's sister, Leah, loves rules and keeps track of who follows them. Ethan, tired of being taunted by rebellious kids for following the rules, joins their mischief. While he has fun for a while, he later feels guilty for what he's done. He learns the hard way that rules are there for his protection.